DOGTOWN

DOGTOWN

Katherine Applegate
and Gennifer Choldenko

With illustrations by Wallace West

FEIWEL AND FRIENDS
New York

A Feiwel and Friends Book
An imprint of Macmillan Publishing Group, LLC
120 Broadway, New York, NY 10271 • mackids.com

Our books may be purchased in bulk for promotional, educational,
or business use. Please contact your local bookseller or the Macmillan
Corporate and Premium Sales Department at (800) 221-7945 ext. 5442
or by email at MacmillanSpecialMarkets@macmillan.com.

Library of Congress Cataloging-in-Publication Data is available.

First edition, 2023
Book design by Michelle Gengaro-Kokmen
The artist used a combination of collage and digital techniques to
create the illustrations for this book.
Feiwel and Friends logo designed by Filomena Tuosto
Printed in the United States of America by Lakeside Book Company,
Harrisonburg, Virginia

ISBN 978-1-250-81160-8 (hardcover)
1 3 5 7 9 10 8 6 4 2
ISBN 978-1-250-32438-2 (international edition)
1 3 5 7 9 10 8 6 4 2

For Suzanne Applegate, my mom, dog lover
extraordinaire, with love –K.A.

For Sharon Levin
Thank you for sharing your love of books
with everyone around you. Thank you for making
me feel like my books matter. –G.C.

chapter
1
Three-Legged Dog

I know what you're thinking: That poor dog only has three legs. But don't go there. It's not that bad, okay?

So, I'm not American Kennel Club material. Big deal.

My eyes are sharp, my nose is wet, my coat puppy soft, and the white patch over my eye?

It's a charmer, I don't mind saying.

My name is Chance. I'm pleased to meet you.

chapter
2
Chance

Something else about me . . . I think about things more than your average pooch. While other dogs are chasing sticks and squirrels, I sit back and appraise the situation. When you hop everywhere you go, each trip takes time. So, you think about where you're heading and why.

Also, three is a lucky number.

Three acts in a play.

Three legs in a stool.

Three times a charm and all of that. And since Management at Dogtown plays a lot of poker, being lucky is pretty darn lucky.

'Course I wasn't lucky when I lost my leg. But that's a story I don't like to tell.

chapter
3
A Place for Homeless Dogs

Dogtown is a shelter—a place for homeless dogs.

The dogs of Dogtown are as fancy as you'll find anywhere. Collies and corgis, shar-peis and sheepdogs, oodles of schnoodles, poodles and labradoodles . . . plus plenty of mutts like me.

And then there are the dogs who aren't dogs at all, because they're made entirely of metal.

Ever petted a stapler? Hugged a toaster? Cuddled a bag of doorknobs?

Then you know what it's like to have a robot dog.

No fun at all.

Why were metal dogs at Dogtown in the first place? That's the question.

chapter
4
Dogtown 2.0

It was Management's idea.

Dogtown 2.0 was a gimmick . . . a publicity stunt.

People loved seeing real dogs roughhousing with robot dogs, tussling and tug-of-warring, sniffing hind ends, or curled up together to rest and recharge.

Newspapers wrote articles. Videos went viral. The evening news ran the story two days in a row.

People came to Dogtown in droves.

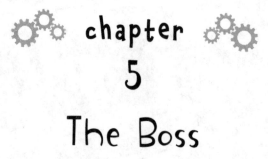

chapter 5

The Boss

Unfortunately, a lot of the folks who visited Dogtown 2.0 went home with robot dogs. Oh the excuses they had!

They were clean freaks.

They were cat people.

They were allergic.

They didn't like dogs who pooped.

That's when the hostility between us real dogs—the flesh-and-bloods—and the metal dogs began.

But Dogtown 2.0 created so much foot traffic that real dog adoptions increased, too.

At least that's what Management said, and she's the boss, right?

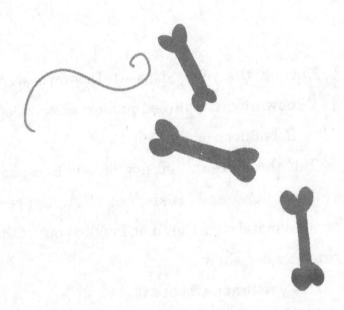

Plug-in Pooches

Most of the robot dogs at Dogtown were known by their breed names: eDog, iDog, Aibo, RoboRover, or Pup 1000.

But those aren't real dog breeds like pugs and pointers and Pekingese. Nothing real about a metal dog. They'd be laughed out of the ring at a dog show.

They're brands. That's it.

Besides that, lots of them are in bad shape by the time they get to Dogtown. Tails broken, wires poking out, chargers missing. Nothing sadder than a plug-in pooch who can't wag his own tail. He'd go straight to the e-waste heap.

Even in her finest hour, no e-dog has a heart. They don't have the first idea of what it feels like to carry one around in your chest. The weight of it, you know?

Metal Head

Robot dogs are expensive, so they generally aren't donated to Dogtown until something stops working. A busted motor, a frozen screen, bugs in the software. That kind of thing.

But Metal Head didn't look damaged. He looked strange, like he'd been put together by a mad scientist. There was something off about his whole backside, as if another dog's rear end was attached to his front end. And he had this

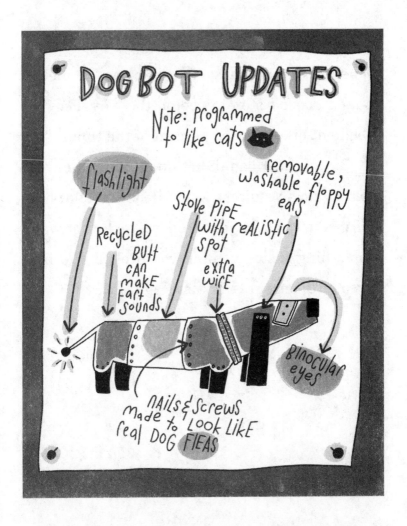

flashing going on that drove us all crazy. Blue flash! Blue flash! Blue flash! All night long. Just looking at him gave me a headache.

It wasn't like he was well-trained, either. When a human says, "Doggy, come," a metal hound doesn't stop to pee on the way. They're obedient one hundred percent of the time.

But Metal Head didn't do anything he was told to do. We didn't know if he was flat-out disobedient. Or he just didn't care. Either way, something inside of him was broken. We figured he'd be sent to e-waste right away.

8

First Cage

We were wrong. Management didn't stick Metal Head in e-waste. She put him in First Cage—the first pen adopting families see when they come to Dogtown.

The first pup they lay eyes on melts their hearts and gets adopted right away.

None of us was happy that a hunk of steel with the personality of a paperweight had been given that premier piece of real estate.

Geraldine, a Saint Bernard, was really ticked

off. (She got sent to Dogtown because—how do I put this delicately?—her piles were too large. I don't understand humans. Doesn't seem that difficult to figure out. Big dog. Big . . .)

Anyhoo, Geraldine wouldn't stop barking about Metal Head getting First Cage. "What am I, kibble dust? All I'm asking for is a little respect, people," she barked.

But the humans didn't understand a word she said. Trying to bridge the human/dog divide is a game of charades. We understand them. They don't understand us.

We joined Geraldine in her Big Bark the way we always do.

But it did no good. Metal Head was going to blink blue in First Cage until Management moved him. There was nothing we could do about it.

chapter 9

Boohoo

If that wasn't bad enough, Metal Head was a boohoo.

Plenty of flesh-and-blood dogs are boohoos. Dogtown is a shelter, after all. Dogs end up in Dogtown because they're lost or abandoned.

They come to us because they bit the mail carrier.

Or they dug up the peonies, the poppies, and the pansies.

Or—and this is a really big no-no—they ate

their human's cell phone. (You wouldn't believe the talented dogs that are dumped because of phone chewing. It's a crying shame.)

Real dogs aren't happy when they arrive. They whine, they whimper, they hide their heads, and refuse to eat. They're hopeful there's a sign stapled to a telephone pole somewhere that says MISSING DOG with their picture on it. Might even offer a reward.

If only they could escape.

If only they could go home.

If only their humans knew where they were.

I couldn't blame them. Who didn't miss home? Cats to chase, kids to race, and a bowl with your name on it.

But in the end, real dogs are resilient. We get over our heartbreak most of the time.

I wasn't so sure about e-dogs. Metal Head was the first one I ever saw who was a boohoo.

Looking back now, I see that was a sign. But at the time, I just figured the guy must have had a power outage at an important stage in his development.

chapter 10
The Manual

Most robot dogs had their instructions built into the circuitry. But Metal Head was old school. He came with a manual. And he was always looking up one thing or another. Never seemed to be satisfied by what he found.

It was like he was looking for something that wasn't there.

He didn't care that he was in First Cage. He paid no attention to the families who walked by. The cutest little girl with dimples, a missing front tooth, and a bag of dog toys bigger than she was stopped smack in front of him. She was jumping up and down, her curly hair springing and spronging.

"Here doggy," she said, offering him one toy after another.

Metal Head didn't even look up.

Next came twin boys with matching outfits. "Doggy! Let us pet you. Pleeeeeeease!" they said.

Then they started doing their routines. Mambos. Moonwalks. Macarenas. Imagine humans doing tricks for dogs!

Metal Head didn't notice. I assumed he was out of charge, until I saw his blue light flashing.

"Sit! Shake! Roll over!" the human kids called out.

They were especially adorable that day. These were families any dog would have been proud to call their own.

chapter
11
Heartless

Robot dogs are obedient. They don't have a choice. Nothing inside them but code.

The fact that Metal Head didn't care about the kids wasn't all that unusual. It just showed he was as heartless as the next hunk of steel.

Still, it was weird he didn't obey.

chapter
12
The Basement

Everybody thought Management would move Metal Head to the basement, which is what we called the pens in the underground room. No dog liked the basement because the cages were small, dark, and cold. And the stairs to the basement were hard to find, so not many adopting families went down there.

I suspected Metal Head would go to the e-waste pile. Never saw a dog fall from First Cage to e-waste, but it could happen.

That's what I was hoping for. Metal Head bugged me. While the rest of us were trying to perfect our adopt-me routines, he was reading his manual.

He upset Geraldine. She had arthritis, so her adopt-me routine was hard on her. She'd wiggle her bottom, walk on her hind legs, then curtsy to her audience. She creaked and groaned, but she did her routine anyway. It was hard for her to understand why Metal Head wouldn't even try.

"Hey, Sugar, you with the metal head," she called to him, "you got to get yourself a routine. Otherwise, you'll never leave this place. Come on, dog, I can help you."

Metal Head ignored her. Wouldn't even turn his head in her direction.

"Did they flip his switch?" Geraldine whispered to me.

"Nope. He's just rude."

Geraldine circled around and around then collapsed on the cement with a big thump. "A dog machine. Whoever heard of such a thing?" she asked.

"Apparently they make one that comes with fake poop," I said.

"Oh for goodness' sakes . . . what's the world coming to, Chance?"

You can see why none of us had much affection

for metal hounds. We'd been burned too many times. We'd do our adopt-me routines: the licks, the tricks, the puppy eyes. And then, when we had a family hooked, the hope would kick in.

We'd imagine car trips with our noses out the windows, bacon in our bowls, belly rubs, and cuddles on the couch. After being petted and played with and loved all up, we'd get excited . . . only to have a family adopt a mound of metal with an on-off switch.

Nothing more than a device, really.

chapter 13

No Hairballs

We'd be left alone on the same cement floor, staring at the same chain-link fence, eating the same cheap kibble out of the same chewed-up bowl.

Metal dogs were easier. That's all there was to it.

No muddy paws.

No sharp claws.

No fleas.

No ticks.

No hairballs.

No vet bills.

No pee stains on the carpet.

No smelly dog food cans in the refrigerator.

No neighbors calling the police because *That dog is barking again*.

No hassles at all.

chapter
14

The Barking Problem

It took the better part of a week, but when Metal Head rejected yet another family, Management moved him to the basement.

Then she switched Geraldine to cage twenty-two. All her barking had gotten the big girl demoted.

This is the problem with barking. It's how we communicate. We bark to tell humans how we feel, and they punish us.

Is that fair or what?

chapter
15
Geraldine

Metal Head got what he deserved. Geraldine did not.

We all loved Geraldine. She was a good listener. She never fell asleep while you were talking or interrupted a heart-to-heart by shoving a ball in your face.

Right then, Geraldine was nudging her water bowl under the fence so my buddy Buster could have a drink. Buster, an enthusiastic ball dog, had knocked his bowl over again.

"You thirsty, Buster?" Geraldine asked. "Just don't tip it over, okay, dog?"

"Thanks, thanks," the golden retriever slobbered between sloppy sips.

The problem was Geraldine had been at Dogtown even longer than I had. Many of the adopting families stopped by her pen, but nobody wanted to take her home. She was too big, too old, and too set in her ways. And we were all worried she was on The List.

Have I told you about The List? Yeah, well I'm not telling you now. I don't want to talk about it. Nobody does.

chapter 🐾 16

Group Howl

Buster was the most upset about Geraldine. And that got him in a heap of trouble, but before I can tell you about that, I have to explain about Buster.

Goldens are usually well-behaved. But not Buster. He slobbered on the floor. He peed on his bones. He drank from the toilet.

He got adopted a lot, on account of everybody loves goldens. But Buster was a bounceback—a dog that gets adopted, then returned. Last time he came back it was because he'd growled at Grandma.

To be fair, she didn't look like any grandma he'd ever seen. She was a six-foot-two bodybuilder with big, black metal-toed boots. And she tiptoed into the bedroom where Buster's little human was sleeping.

She only wanted to hug her grandson goodnight. "How, how was I supposed to know that?" Buster asked when he told me the story.

Good question.

There is one more thing about Buster. If Buster likes you, he LIKES YOU. I'd seen him take on three mastiffs and a Maltese because they were picking on a dog he cared about.

But if Buster didn't like you. Watch out.

Buster loved Geraldine, so the first thing he did was throw himself against his chain-link fence. He banged, he bounced, he boomeranged back, and he barked his head off. And then he got us started on a Group Howl to complain about Geraldine's move to cage twenty-two. That made us feel a little better.

A good howl always does.

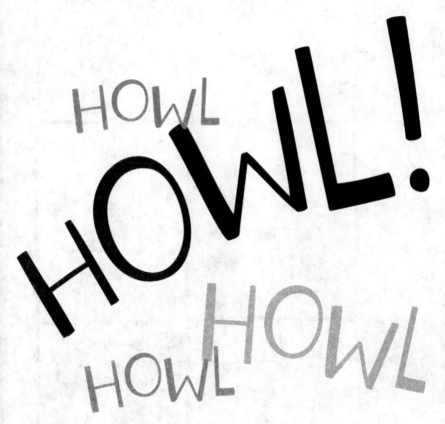

chapter
17
Off the Books

The neighbors complained about the howling. And Management knew Buster had started it. Plus Buster had thrown himself at the fence so many times it was all bent up. So, Management sent him down to the basement, to the pen next to Metal Head. Management tried to anyway, but Buster wouldn't budge. She had to get four volunteers to carry him out.

Since my best friend and Buster were both in the basement, I hopped down the stairs to visit every afternoon.

Wait. I forgot to tell you how come I got to go wherever I wanted, didn't I?

Well, here's the truth. Nobody is going to adopt a three-legged mutt. The way I move, all hoppity, hoppity . . . I'm a pity party in a dog suit, okay? Sunbathing on the beach, pet parades, and picnics in the park . . . regular stuff a human might enjoy with their dog wouldn't be fun with me. Everybody would be asking: "What happened to your dog? Why is she missing a leg?"

Yeah. So. No.

But since I was Management's lucky charm, I had the run of Dogtown. I didn't take up space because I wasn't assigned a cage, which helped me stay off The List.

I was "off the books" for nearly seven months, which is four years in dog time, if you're still using the one-to-seven-years rule.

chapter 18

Just Out of the Dishwasher

So I headed down to the basement to see Buster and have dinner with my friend, Mouse.

Buster spent a lot of time in the basement, which was really tough on him because the pens were small for a dog with his energy.

"Wanna, wanna play ball, Chance?" Buster asked when he saw me.

There was a gap between the floor and the bottom of the pen. Just enough room to roll a ball under.

It wasn't much of a game, but we enjoyed it. When we took a break, Buster asked: "What's happening happening with Geraldine?"

I passed the ball back. "Been kind of quiet, and that's not good."

"No, oh no, no, no." Buster kicked the ball, pounced on it, drooled over it, and pinged it under the fence. "What are we gonna gonna do?"

"I'm working on it, Buster," I said, breathing in Buster's smell: steak bones and hairballs, and another scent . . . like silverware just out of the dishwasher.

Wait. That was coming from Metal Head's pen next door. I looked over at him. He was busy reading his manual as usual.

I walked closer. I liked the smell of silverware out of the dishwasher. It reminded me of home.

"Ball, Chance, ball, ball, ball," Buster barked.

"Sorry, Buster," I said, passing the ball back. "I can't play anymore. I've got things to do."

"One more, one, one, one," Buster begged.

I hated to disappoint him, but it was time to move on.

chapter 19

Humans Don't Speak Dog

Metal Head's eyes were on me. "How does one get out of here?" he asked in Human English.

I didn't know if he meant out of his pen, out of the basement, or out of Dogtown.

Whatever the question, the answer was complicated, and I didn't feel like playing charades, so I shook my head.

Metal Head asked again . . . this time in Dog.

I did a double take. Nearly lost my kennel ration.

Metal dogs didn't know Dog. How could they? They were programmed by humans, and humans don't speak Dog.

"How'd you learn Dog?" I asked.

"I pay attention," he said. "And now I wish to know how to leave this place."

"Oh, that's easy. You get adopted."

Metal Head walked up to the fence. "No, I mean on my own."

"Escape? Forget it. No way out for a dog, or whatever you are."

"You call me 'Metal Head,'" he said.

"Yeah, I know," I mumbled. I was starting to feel pretty lousy right then. I'd been saying things about Metal Head that I'd never have told him to his face. It hadn't occurred to me he understood Dog.

I learned something important that day: Never say something about a dog that you wouldn't want him to hear.

"I like the moniker," Metal Head said.

I didn't know if he'd burned out his bulbs or somebody had adjusted his settings, but the blue flashing had stopped. I could look at him without getting a headache.

"Why do you want to escape?" I asked.

"I want to go home," he said.

chapter 20
Doggy Amnesia

Now I understood. Every boohoo in Dogtown said "I want to go home" at one time or another. They couldn't grasp how their precious, pampered selves could have been tossed out.

They chose not to remember the half-eaten homework, the paw prints on the pillow, the torn tablecloth, the wedding dress missing one sleeve. The fact that they preferred to piddle on the bathroom rug . . . that slipped their minds, too.

Doggy amnesia, we called it.

I told Metal Head what I said to all boohoos. "It's never going to happen."

"I think you're mistaken," he said.

I shook my head. "You can't get out of your cage, much less out of the basement. Forget escaping from Dogtown. Even if that were possible, you can't walk all the way back to your house. And if, by some miracle, you managed that, they don't want you back. That's why they left you here."

I waited for him to say he'd gotten lost. It is the no-fault reason they all come up with.

But Metal Head simply said, "I need your assistance. The little guy listens to you." He pointed with his big metal nose toward Mouse's house, up high in the rafters.

I shrugged. I wasn't about to get my best buddy involved in Metal Head's crazy plans.

All the boohoos wanted to run away. They got over it. Metal Head would wake up and smell the dog biscuits, just like every other boohoo before him.

And that would be the end of the running-away plan.

chapter 21
First Night

To understand what happened next, you need to know how Mouse and I became friends.

I arrived at Dogtown last winter. A new snow had fallen, and there was a howling wind that bit through my fur. Even a husky needed a parka in the bitter cold we were having.

Management took one look at me and tossed me in a cage at the back of the basement. She knew from experience that nobody wants a dog with three legs.

The plan was to wait until enough time went by and they could put me on The List.

I didn't know that then. I had no idea there was such a thing as a list, but I know now.

Like every other newcomer to Dogtown, my heart was broken. I missed curling up in the furry blanket at the foot of Jessie's bed. I missed the jingle of my leash and the squeak of the school bus door when Jessie came home. I missed pepperoni pizza, pulled pork, and chasing pigeons in the park. But mostly I missed Jessie and Professor Besser.

I slept during the day and stared out the tiny basement window at night. I memorized the stars and grew familiar with the train whistles. I could tell the time of day by the sound of the toots.

Dogtown had heat, only it didn't work very well in the basement. It felt like minus twenty-five. My kibbles were popsicles, my water bowl had iced over, and the cement floor was like an ice-skating rink.

So I did what dogs all over the world do when we're unhappy.

I barked.

But all I got for my trouble was a sore throat.

❖ chapter ❖
22
Bad Speller

Those were terrible days. Worse than the cold was the loneliness.

I woke up hearing my little Jessie calling my name. I imagined her so clearly, Jessie, with the fuzzy pigtails and a smile so radiant that every dog in the dog park ran to her.

I pined for Jessie's mother, Professor Besser.

I ached to have my belly rubbed, my fur stroked, my left ear massaged in that special way.

Even when Management came by, it was only for a moment or two. With a hundred dogs to care for and nowhere near enough help, they could barely keep up with the basics: Food. Water. Cage cleaning.

Now and then, they'd pat me on the head. But a belly rub?

Too many bellies, not enough minutes in the day.

I wondered if I had enough kibble left in my bowl to write a note. Spelling has never been my strong suit. My grammar is not so hot, either. In Human, anyway. I'm fluent in Dog.

I moved the kibble around until I had my message. But then the wind gusted down the corridor and blew away the pellets that read: *I nid to b petd.*

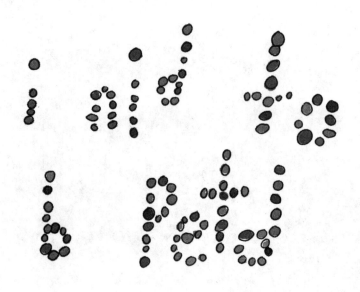

chapter 23

Volunteers

I ran into a few dogs at Dogtown who'd done time in other shelters. They claimed Dogtown wasn't half bad compared to those places, mostly because there were so many volunteers who helped out.

The volunteers were all right. I mean, what kind of person *volunteers* to pick up poop?

You could smell the kindness on those people.

Also the dog poop.

And Management? She was doing the best she could. But she was outnumbered.

There are a whole lot of unwanted dogs in the world, it seems.

58

chapter
24
Suppertime

Suppertime was the worst. I'd always eaten my supper with the Bessers in the TV room. I wasn't used to eating alone. I missed the blueberry pancake smell of Jessie and the toasted almonds and manila folder smell of Professor Besser.

That was back when I hadn't given up hope I'd see Jessie and Professor Besser again. Back then, every footstep sounded like theirs. Every person looked like them. Every time the basement door opened, I was sure it was them.

Mostly what I heard was the whistle of the train and the clanking of the railroad crossing gates. I looked out at the long row of empty cages. And I breathed in the bitter ammonia of loneliness.

I did all the usual things to keep myself occupied. I scratched my ears. I gnawed my paws. I cleaned my private parts. And I dreamed of

my bowl at the Bessers', full of dumplings and drippings, burgers and bacon, chicken bites and big chunks of chili beef.

Dogtown kibble tasted like tree bark. I couldn't eat it.

I'd just begun chewing the chain-link when a small brown mouse made a dash for my dish.

I jumped up, my hackles raised. But at the last second, I held my growl. It had been such a long time since I'd been near another creature.

I suddenly realized I was happy to share the contents of my kibble bowl.

What was the harm?

chapter
25
Mouse

Mouse lived in a safe little hideaway above cage ninety-one. Management didn't know about Mouse's house because she didn't like schlepping down to the basement any more than anybody else did.

Mouse wasn't jumpy the way most mice are. And he was exceptionally intelligent. He knew how to read and he was trilingual (Mouse, Human, Dog), and besides that he was crafty. He could get anywhere in Dog-town without being seen.

That night I watched him set about the busi-ness of rolling kibble across the cement to the back of the pen. Then, one by one, he'd take them in his mouth, climb the chain-link to the knothole in the corner, and disappear inside. A minute later he'd appear again, scramble down, retrieve another kibble, and climb back up.

He made five trips, then nodded his thanks and disappeared into the knothole door.

I hadn't eaten much since I'd ar-rived at Dogtown. But seeing another creature's interest in my dinner made me hungry. I finished all of my kibble that night.

Mouse was small, so I figured five kibble bits would last the better part of a week. But the next day he was back.

That's when I figured out he was feeding a whole lot of other mice up there.

I looked forward to Mouse's visits. Every day I would wait for him to come down, take his five kibbles, and nod his thank-you. And every evening, his visit gave me back my appetite.

It doesn't sound like much. But Mouse, the train whistles, and the stars in the night sky got me through the long winter in Dogtown.

chapter 26

Puppy Season

Spring is puppy whelping season. That means lots of puppies are born in Dogtown or dropped off in wooden crates or cardboard boxes. Puppies can't be adopted until they're eight weeks old, so new dog moms were assigned to the basement. Soon puppy yips and yaps, whines and whimpers rang through the air.

We had litters of peekapoos, pugapoos, cockapoos, and havapoos.

And yet more came.

What would Management do with all those dogs?

Then Buster had another bounceback. I can't remember if that was the time he chewed the teacher's gradebook, or ate an entire wedding cake. Maybe it was when he peed in the heater vent and the whole house smelled like the side of a fire hydrant all winter long.

Anyhoo, Buster was back, and explained to me about The List.

"Ever wonder what happens happens to the dogs that don't get adopted?" he had asked.

What was he was talking about? The dogs that didn't get adopted just stayed in Dogtown, didn't they? But when I looked over at him, he was doing a trick I'd never seen him do before.

He was playing dead.

That's when I began to put the pieces of the Milk-Bone together.

chapter 27

Lucky Dog

I mentioned that Management liked to play poker. But I don't think I told you how serious they were about it. Every Wednesday after work, all the Dogtown humans sat in the back room with their heads hunched over their cards. There were big stacks of poker chips, pizza, pretzels, and potato chips piled all around.

So, there I was, thinking I'd been at Dogtown too long. Management had me on The

List. I was headed for the great dog park in the sky when something strange happened.

The three of hearts showed up on my cage. The card was stuck in the chain-link. When Management saw it, she came thundering out to my pen, followed by Front Desk and three volunteers. No one could figure out how the three of hearts got from the back room to the basement. Or why it was there.

On Tuesday, the three of spades appeared in the same place the three of hearts had been. On Wednesday, it was the three of diamonds.

By then, there was a real hullabaloo. Front Desk's girlfriend, Management's husband, and a bunch of volunteers and their kids came to see me.

"Look at her!" A volunteer who smelled like bananas pointed at me. "She's posing by the cards."

Okay, that was true. Who doesn't like to feel special?

Front Desk's girlfriend rolled her eyes. "You do know it's not possible for a dog to open her pen, go into the back room, get a deck of cards, find all the threes, and stick them in the fence, right?"

"Let us have our fun," Front Desk whispered.

Front Desk's girlfriend snorted. "You guys are out of your minds."

"Don't you believe in luck?" a tall volunteer with peanut butter breath asked.

Front Desk's girlfriend shook her head. "This has nothing to do with luck."

"Well, I could use some good luck," Front Desk announced. "Hey, I have an idea. We could give Chance the run of the place and spread the luck around."

A little girl stuck her sticky fingers through the fence and I cleaned them off for her. "Everyone could get a lucky lick," she said.

Peanut butter breath opened the pen so I could come out. "Friendliest dog here."

"I thought it was just me she liked," another volunteer said when I nuzzled her.

Peanut butter breath squatted down to pet me. "That's her genius. She makes everyone feel like her favorite."

"You can't let her run free," Management's husband said. "She'll run away."

"Have you seen her move? She's not going anywhere," Front Desk said.

Management ran her hand over my head. "I suppose we could give

71

it a try, but poker night she sits with me."

So that's how I got the run of the place and a home under the poker table.

Lucky for them.

Lucky for me.

There isn't a dog in the world that doesn't have a little watchdog in her. And I am no exception.

So yes, I did know how the cards appeared in the chain-link. Which is why every suppertime I hopped down the stairs to the basement with a mouthful of kibble for Mouse.

Here's another thing humans are sadly misguided about: Luck is not a winning hand of cards. Luck is making a new friend.

Dog Language

All dogs are bilingual. We understand the language our humans speak and our Dog language.

Mouse as I mentioned was trilingual, but without the proper voice box required for speech, Mouse uses sign language to communicate his thoughts.

Mouse learned all of this growing up in Dogtown.

But Metal Head didn't grow up in Dogtown

or anywhere else for that matter. Metal dogs don't get older or wiser. One day you plug them in and that's it.

So how come Metal Head spoke Dog? He had said it was because he paid attention. But I didn't see how a metal dog could learn the way we do. And if they could, then we are in big trouble.

If metal dogs became more real, then where would that leave us?

30

Real Dogs Only

The best days at Dogtown were Reading Buddy days.

The Reading Buddy program was designed to help human children get more confident with their reading. But for us, it was so much more.

Like I said, most of us Dogtowners got very little cuddling. There were too many dogs and too much for the volunteers to do. But on Reading Buddy days, we got visits from the cutest kids around. We sat in their laps, nuzzled their knees, and listened while books with bright, beautiful pictures were read to us.

Even the grouchiest dog in Dogtown wagged his tail on Reading Buddy days.

Mouse loved Reading Buddies as much as we did. He had dozens of hiding places by the book baskets on Reading Buddy Row, and he had a favorite book called *Charlotte's Web*. That's how Mouse learned to read, as a matter of fact.

Metal dogs got to be Reading Buddies, too. But few kids wanted to cuddle with a machine, or curl up next to an electrical outlet.

The kids loved hanging out with real dogs. The parents loved seeing photos of their kid reading to a dog. And Management loved taking pictures for the website.

Win-win for everyone.

And once in a while, a dog got adopted by her Reading Buddy. It had happened enough times to get a dog's hopes up.

Even a dog like me.

31

Reading Buddy Row

Reading Buddy Row had spacious pens, good AC in the summer, and central heat in the winter. It was the nicest section of Dogtown.

Every dog wanted to be there.

But earning a spot on Reading Buddy Row wasn't easy.

Dancing, prancing, howling, growling, or sleeping during story time were all big no-nos. Dogs like Buster couldn't sit still. They wanted to play ball! Ball! Ball! Other dogs were kicked out for snoring, growling at the villains, or covering their eyes during the scary parts. The kids understood what we were doing, but the grown-ups did not.

Geraldine and I liked to bark to warn the heroes where the villain was hiding. We weren't exactly booted out of Reading Buddies, but we weren't asked back, either.

Metal dogs didn't have these problems. Metal dogs sat like fence posts while the kids read to them.

chapter 32

Quinn

Mr. Molinari was our favorite teacher. He had a biscuit for every dog. And a kind word for every student. He understood Reading Buddies really well, so almost all of the kids in Mr. Molinari's class found a Reading Buddy right away.

Often, they picked a Jack Russell terrier named Bear. Bear had an earnest listening expression: ears perked, eyes wide, tail wagging. The kids adored him. I watched Bear to see how it was done, but I could not get the hang of it.

The big dogs were also good Reading Buddies. Some of them anyway. Get a couple of Newfies and a Mastiff in there and you needed a gas mask . . . you know what I'm saying?

Anyhoo, there was this one kid, Quinn, who couldn't find a book to read or a dog to read it to. Quinn had hair combed in a direction hair was not meant to go and glasses that sat crooked on his head. His left shoe was generally untied, and he wore the same shirt every time we saw him. It had a picture of a star on it.

Quinn would go up and down Reading Buddy Row searching for a dog. Then he'd take out every book in every basket searching for a story. But he could find neither. By the end of the hour, he'd be sitting in the corner all by himself.

Since I was still hopeful Management would give me another try at Reading Buddies, I hopped over to him and gave him a good sniff. He smelled terrific. Like buttered toast with a touch of toothpaste.

A smell like that and you'll go far in life.

I took an immediate liking to him, so I dug through the book basket until I found a book about toast. I dragged it over to him, then settled back to hear the story.

But Quinn didn't touch the book. This was not the one.

Then I got another brainstorm. Quinn's shirt had a star on it. I hopped to every basket until I found a book on the solar system.

Yeah, I had it now. I'm so clever sometimes.

But Quinn had no more interest in the book about the solar system than he had in the book about toast.

Clearly, it was time to deploy my secret weapon.

chapter
33

The Three-Legged Show

I did my act.

The tri-pawed juggle.

The hug and snuggle.

A dog plays dead.

A ball on my head.

And a one-pawed spin just for Quinn.

But I was wasting my time. Quinn couldn't have cared less.

About then, Management stepped in. Someone from the local news had shown up, and there was Quinn, sitting all by himself. It was a public relations disaster.

Management walked Quinn past all the available dogs, but Quinn had no use for any of them.

When Mr. Molinari saw what was going on, he said, "Leave Quinn be. He'll figure it out."

chapter
34

Buttered Toast with Toothpaste

Quinn didn't figure it out.

Week after week, he roamed from one end of the main building to the other. I kept an eye on him. It had been a long time since I'd gotten a whiff of buttered toast.

And buttered toast with toothpaste?

You couldn't get better than that.

I wanted Quinn to like me. I wanted him to pick me, so I tried to figure out what was going on with him. There were kids who didn't like

Reading Buddies because they didn't like dogs, or our books were too easy, or they didn't get enough recess that day. But Quinn wasn't like any of these kids.

Quinn was searching for something. I just didn't know what.

chapter

35

Wandering

Then one day Quinn's wandering took him down to the basement.

Buster saw him first. He wagged his tail so hard it banged the pen. Two Scotties named Phil and Lil fell all over each other in a frenzy of excitement. Bill, the beagle, whipped around in circles. Shag, the sheepdog, jumped up, banging his big paws on the fence, which sent great clouds of white hair drifting like snow to the ground.

Quinn walked by all of them.

But then at cage ninety-two, he slowed down.

Metal Head.

Metal Head didn't wag his tail. He didn't stick his nose through the fence or dance on his hind legs. He didn't even look up.

Quinn stared at him, rocking from foot to foot. Then he sat down.

All he needed was a book. The problem was, Reading Buddies didn't go to the basement, so there weren't any book baskets in there. For me to go all the way up to the main building, grab a book between my teeth, and hop back down to the basement would take too long.

Reading Buddies would be over by then.

chapter 36

Books by Heart

I couldn't remember what day Metal Head had arrived. I didn't know if he'd seen Reading Buddies in action. All I could think to say was: "You wouldn't happen to know any books by heart, would you, Metal Head?"

Metal Head looked from me to Quinn. Then back at me, then back at Quinn. Finally, he opened his mouth and said, "I am Sam. Sam I am."

When Quinn heard this, his eyes grew large.

His hands flapped as he jumped up and took off like he was chasing a deer.

chapter 37
Something Big

When Quinn came back, he was clutching a book.

He ran straight to cage ninety-two with Mr. Molinari and Management on his heels. Quinn sat down and looked at Metal Head. And Metal Head looked right back.

Quinn opened *Green Eggs and Ham* and turned the pages as Metal Head said the words.

"That Sam-I-am

I do not like that Sam-I-am."

It wasn't the way it was supposed to be, with the kid reading and the dog listening. But one look at Metal Head and Quinn, scooted up close to each other, and it was pretty clear something had happened.

Something big.

chapter 38
A Metal Heart

After that, I figured Metal Head would get over his boohoos and settle down like the rest of us. Boy, was I wrong. The next time I saw him he called out, "What about *your* humans, Chance? Don't *you* want to go home?"

This was not the kind of question Dogtown dogs asked each other. If a dog wanted to talk about how she ended up at Dogtown, that was fine. But you didn't ask a question that broke a dog's heart to answer.

How do you explain kindness to a machine with a hunk of metal where his heart should've been?

I really didn't know.

chapter
39
Mixed Feelings

There had been complaints about Metal Head. Not everybody liked that Quinn had chosen him. And because I had the run of the place, I was the dog who handled dog fights when they arose. So, I hopped over to his cage to have a talk with him.

Before I could open my mouth, Metal Head repeated his question: "What about your humans? You're not locked up. Why don't you go find them?"

"It's complicated," I explained.

"What's complicated about going home?" he asked.

Everything is black or white for a dog machine. A one or a zero. There's no room for nuance. No understanding of delicate situations.

And mixed feelings? Forget about them.

40

Fake Fleas

Metal Head turned over and began scratching his belly.

See, this was the weird thing about metal dogs: They came with fake fleas you attached with Velcro. Humans paid extra to see a robot dog scratch his fleas off. Then when company came over, the human attached the fleas and the metal dog scratched them off again.

Fleas, seriously?

It's like building a robot dog that farts. It made no sense.

Metal Head eyed me again. "I don't understand your resistance to speaking with the little guy on my behalf." He pointed his clunky metal paw to the knothole corner above cage ninety-one.

"Talk to him yourself."

"He doesn't pay attention to me," Metal Head said.

I wanted to say, *none of us do*. But I tried to be polite. "Look, the other dogs are a little jealous that Quinn picked you."

"That is not my concern."

"I know. I just think you should keep a low profile is all."

His light blinked blue.

"You still planning an escape?" I asked.

"Yes."

I shrugged this off. No use in giving airtime to nonsense. And there was no way I was going to get Mouse involved. Mouse was roughly the size of a tennis ball. How was he going to help a clunky beast like Metal Head?

I changed the subject to what I'd come to his pen to discuss. "You can't ask dogs about why they're here."

"Why not?"

"Because it's a sore subject."

He shrugged.

"Do you know what that means?" I asked.

No answer.

But when I looked in his glass eyes, I saw a flicker I hadn't seen before. Metal Head was trying to understand.

Was it possible he had a heart he didn't know how to use?

chapter 41

Out of Charge

The next time Quinn came, he ran to the book basket, got *Green Eggs and Ham,* and headed down to the basement.

He was faster than me. Well . . . everybody is faster than me.

They were already halfway through the book when I arrived. That was okay. I knew the story. I just liked to watch Quinn enjoy himself.

Over and over, Metal Head repeated the

words. And over and over, Quinn turned the pages.

After the seventh time through, Metal Head began slowing down. Management had forgotten to charge him. He was saying the words slower and slower and s l o w e r.

"I . . . am . . . Sam . . ."

Quinn didn't like this. He had to wait way too long to turn the page.

I couldn't plug in Metal Head myself. And with so many people around, it would have been dangerous to ask Mouse. Then something else weird happened. Quinn took his finger and tracked each word as Metal Head said it.

And when Metal Head did run out of charge, Quinn kept going.

It wasn't reading, exactly. Quinn had the words memorized.

But it was a start. You could almost see Quinn's mind putting the sounds together with the letters.

In the next few weeks, we saw Quinn mouth the words as Metal Head said them. And then one day Mr. Molinari put all the words in a list, and Quinn read each and every one.

Quinn wasn't a bubbly, smiley kind of kid. Most of the time his expression was as serious as cement. But when he read those words, a light went on inside of him that had not been there before.

chapter 42
I Didn't See It Coming

Not everybody was happy about what was happening between Metal Head and Quinn.

The animosity between real dogs and metal dogs ran deep. Almost every real dog in Dogtown had been passed over in favor of a metal dog.

And though there were other metal dogs who wore Reading Buddy sweaters, none got the attention of Metal Head.

I have to admit I was partly to blame. I'd

seen Quinn struggle for such a long time that I was thrilled when he finally found a buddy. Of course, I would have liked his buddy to have been a real dog, but I wasn't a sore loser.

Just seeing Quinn doing well made me happy.

But not all the dogs felt this way. My excitement only made matters worse.

If only I'd seen it coming.

chapter 43

Bad Liars

I was as surprised as Management about what happened on the next Reading Buddy day. Quinn came roaring up to the book basket to get *Green Eggs and Ham* like he always did . . . but it wasn't there.

He ran for the next basket. Not there.

And the next. And the next.

Not here. Not there. Not anywhere.

Green Eggs and Ham was gone.

Books   disappeared   now   and   then.

Management borrowed a book. The library swapped out a title. A kid took one home.

So, I asked the dogs on Reading Buddy Row: "Do you guys know what happened to *Green Eggs and Ham*?"

But every dog shook his head no.

Dogs are bad liars. Have I mentioned this before? If a dog grabs your butter dish, you hear the crash, you see the entire stick of butter in his mouth. But when you ask him: "Did you steal the butter?" he says no, then skulks away, tail between his legs.

So yeah, I knew the dogs were lying. And Geraldine did, too. "Chance, baby, go easy on him, dog. He meant well," she said.

I didn't need to see the tattered pieces of the cover in Buster's cage to know which dog "meant well."

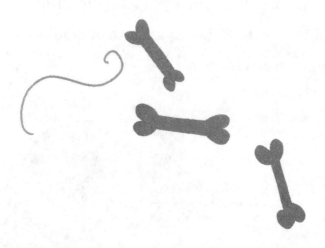

A Happy Accident

Quinn was beside himself. Mr. Molinari did his best to talk him down. "It's a happy accident," he said.

Nothing against Mr. Molinari or anything, but if your bone falls down a storm drain, that's an accident, but it's certainly not happy.

Quinn didn't buy it any more than I did.

So, Management stepped in. She got all up in Quinn's face, suggesting title after title.

Quinn turned red. Then he began shrieking and spinning around.

He was starting to understand the world around him in a way he hadn't before. And the book that had made the difference was gone.

Still, it wasn't okay to behave that way. So, Quinn was suspended from Reading Buddies, which made Mouse and me very sad.

chapter
45
Buster

I was boiling mad at Buster, and I hopped down to the basement to tell him so.

"Wanna wanna play ball, Chance?" Buster asked when he saw me.

"No!"

Buster wagged his tail. "Please please please."

"Why did you chew Quinn's book?" I barked.

Buster's tail stopped wagging. His black nose quivered. "Metal Head took Geraldine's spot spot in First Cage. That was Metal Head's book book."

"First off, that was weeks ago," I said.

Buster's tail slinked down between his legs. "Geraldine needs needs help."

"What you did didn't help Geraldine, it hurt Quinn."

"Oooooooooh." Buster gnawed his paw.

"So now we've got a big mess."

"Uh-oh. UH-OH!" Buster gnawed faster.

"Uh-oh is right," I said.

"Wait! Wait! I know how to fix it." Buster jumped up, burped loudly, and retched until he produced a little white puddle with tiny flecks of orange.

"That's not going to work, Buster. The book's ruined."

"Uh-oh. UH-OH! Won't do it again. Never

ever. Never ever," Buster said, licking up his tiny pool of puke.

Never, ever. How many times had I heard that before? But Geraldine's right about Buster. He wasn't mean or malicious. He was misguided was all.

I sighed. "All right, Buster. But please don't chew any more books."

"Never ever. Never ever," he muttered, chasing the ball around his pen.

Lucky for Buster, he was adopted that day.

Buster was pretty much the only dog that ever got adopted from the basement. But it happened to him regularly. Someone would ask if there were any goldens in Dogtown, and Management would bring Buster up to the front. Then Buster would do his adopt-me

routine. He'd dance on his hind legs, push an imaginary doorbell with his paw, and balance a stack of Milk-Bones on his nose. His finale was two paws on either side of a bent head. He was praying the family would take him home.

It worked every time.

Even though I was still mad at him for chewing up *Green Eggs and Ham,* he was a good friend, and I hoped he'd found his forever home.

But Buster being Buster . . . who knew?

chapter 46

A Yorkie Named Marlene

It was a wild week. First there was the Quinn fiasco. Then a Yorkie named Marlene arrived in Dogtown. Marlene had the worst case of boohoos I'd ever seen. It's tough to get used to a shelter when you've been as pampered as she had been. Marlene had slept on a silk pillow. And she was wheeled around in a baby carriage.

She had dozens of coordinating jackets, hats, and booties, pajamas that matched her

human's, and a costume for every holiday. She even had a Christmas stocking embroidered with her name on it.

Not only that, her human carried diaper wipes and toilet paper in her pocket. You know why, right?

But Marlene's human had gone to the great dog show in the sky. And none of Marlene's relatives wanted to wheel Marlene around in a baby carriage and wipe her tail end with toilet paper. So, she came to us.

Poor Marlene didn't understand that her human wasn't coming back. She kept telling us how sad her human must be without her.

Then Bill, the beagle, told Marlene about the telephone pole signs. After that, all Marlene could talk about was the sign she imagined was out there: MISSING! ADORABLE YORKIE NAMED MARLENE, LAST SEEN WEARING A LEOPARD-PRINT BERET. ONE MILLION DOLLAR REWARD FOR HER RETURN.

According to Marlene, every phone pole in the entire world had a poster with her picture on it. There was simply no convincing her otherwise.

chapter 47

The Boohoos Don't Last

Even without her berets, Marlene was adorable. In less than a week, another lady with an empty baby carriage came through Dogtown and Marlene had a home.

Dogs are resilient. We get over stuff. There's always another bone to find, another ball to chase, another human willing to buy you a leopard-print coat with matching booties.

The boohoos don't last.

chapter 48

My Dinner with Mouse

With all of this going on, I hadn't had time for a leisurely dinner with Mouse in nearly a week. I'd been dropping off his kibble and hurrying back to deal with one calamity after another. Finally, things calmed down enough for us to meet for dinner.

Metal Head generally stayed on the opposite side of his pen, absorbed in his manual. He had a pencil in his mouth, and sometimes he took notes. But that night, his nose was pressed through the chain-link, watching as I arranged the coffee cup lid we used as a table.

"I need your assistance," Metal Head announced as Mouse came out of his knothole house.

I was looking forward to telling Mouse about my day and hearing all about his. But I knew Metal Head wouldn't leave us alone until we let him say his piece, so I nodded that he should continue.

"Could you please procure a leash for me, Chance? The small size they use for toy dogs like Marlene. The little guy"—he pointed with his nose at Mouse—"will carry the leash handle and place it over the latch there. Then I will grasp both ends of the leash with my teeth, pull down, and the latch will open."

What he was asking for was easy enough to do. The leashes were hung on pegs behind the front desk. After closing, I could grab one.

Mouse's part was also relatively simple. Mouse wouldn't have any trouble climbing the chain-link with the leash handle in his mouth.

Even so, I wasn't about to go along.

"What about Quinn?" I asked.

"He's suspended," Metal Head said.

"Yeah, but he'll be back."

"If he does return, then one of you flesh-and-bloods can read to him."

"You know that's not possible," I said.

Metal Head's tail whapped the floor in a

hard, impatient way. "For-give me, but I have important business to attend to."

"I'm not about to help you leave. Quinn needs you," I said.

Metal Head's face was blank, so I couldn't tell what he thought about that. After that he went back to reading his manual and left Mouse and me to enjoy our dinner in peace.

chapter 49
The List

The next day we had a new crisis. It started when I overheard Front Desk calling a Saint Bernard Rescue to see if they could take a seven-year-old Saint Bernard. Only one reason Front Desk would do that.

Geraldine's name was at the top of The List.

Of course, we had protocol for that sort of thing. First the Big Bark. Then the Group Howl.

We hoped our voices would make a difference. At least buy the big dog a few days. But

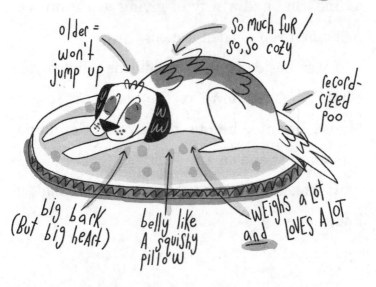

older =
won't
jump up

So much fur/
so, so cozy

record-
sized
poo

big bark
(But big heart)

belly like
a squishy
pillow

weighs a lot
and LOVES A LOT

Management wasn't swayed by the Big Bark or the Group Howl. We'd used them too often.

That's not to say that Management wasn't fond of Geraldine. They spotlighted her on the website, moved her to a pen in the front, and talked to a foster home network about her. When none of this worked, Management began calling her dog-loving friends.

Like I said all of us Dogtowners loved Geraldine. She had a way of giving you a nuzzle just when you needed it most.

I was beside myself, wondering what to do. First, I hopped down to the basement to get Mouse. I wanted him to confirm that Geraldine was number one on The List.

It looked to me like she was. But we had to know for sure.

Robots Don't Get Ideas

When I hoppity hopped by Metal Head's pen, he had his nose in his manual again. He hadn't shown any interest in Geraldine, so I was surprised when he asked about her. "I understand Geraldine is experiencing some difficulties."

"Yup," I said.

"I have a solution for her predicament."

That should have been a clue right there. Robot dogs don't get ideas of their own. They're programmed to do what humans want. But yesterday, Metal Head had proposed his own escape plan. And now he was claiming to have a way to help Geraldine.

I didn't believe it. And I wasn't going to take the time to listen. I kept hopping. Didn't even slow down.

Metal Head barked loudly.

I ignored him. All I could think about was Geraldine.

chapter 51

A Tail-Out

I asked Mouse to run over to the office and check the clipboard, but he shook his head no. Then he pointed at Metal Head.

I motioned for Mouse to hurry, but he crossed his arms and glared at me, his tail thumping the ground. For a little guy, he sure was stubborn.

I gave up and hopped over to find out what Metal Head was yapping about.

"I've been trying to tell you, I know how

we can assist Geraldine. Please hear me out," Metal Head said.

"I'm all ears," I said.

"If I share my idea with you, will you and the little guy assist me in my pursuit?" Metal Head asked.

I considered my answer carefully. I didn't want Metal Head to leave Quinn. Quinn needed him, and I knew Quinn would be back. But I couldn't stand to lose Geraldine, either.

"If your idea works. If it saves Geraldine," I said.

Metal Head nodded and we touched noses, which is how dogs promise.

"We need to initiate a tail-out. Get everyone involved," Metal Head said.

"A what?" I asked.

"A tail-out. When Dogtown opens tomorrow, every dog turns away from the patrons. No tricks. No nuzzling. No puppy eyes. If a human gets close, we growl. Only Geraldine is friendly. Only Geraldine does her act. Only Geraldine sticks her nose through the fence, licks and loves up the humans."

This was a lot to ask. It meant all the dogs in Dogtown would have to give up their dreams of finding a forever home. Just for one day . . . but still.

Maybe it was a trick? An opportunity for the robot dogs to get the upper hand?

"What about the other e-dogs? Can you get them on board?" I asked.

"Probably better if we get Mouse to unplug them."

My mouth dropped open. What a brilliant

idea! Management plugged them in every night. Why not unplug them?

"Do we have a deal?" he asked.

"Yes," I said, touching noses again. "We do."

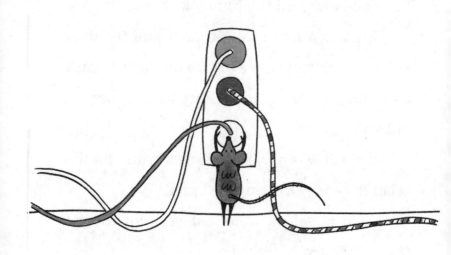

chapter 52
Diva of Dogtown

Most of the humans who came to Dogtown wanted a little dog. Only a few were looking for a big dog. Especially a two-hundred-and-twenty-pounder like Geraldine.

Nobody wanted an old dog either. Old dogs had big vet bills, they were set in their ways, and they didn't have long to live. If they got a puppy, they'd have him for ten, twelve, fifteen years. If they got an old dog, it might be only one or two.

But Metal Head's idea was the only one we had, so I threw my heart into making it work.

Getting all the dogs on board would be a tall order. Every dog woke up in the morning dreaming of being chosen. Nobody wanted to give up that chance.

I started with Geraldine's best buddies. Trooper, the mastiff, was all in before I even got the question out. I wasn't surprised. We all suspected Trooper had a thing for Geraldine.

Soon all the big dogs had signed on. The

reception was surprisingly good with the medium-size dogs, too. They looked up to the big dogs.

Everybody said yes, until I got to Dasha, the Diva of Dogtown. Dasha, an Irish setter, had been a show dog once. She spent most of her day grooming herself, and telling anyone who would listen about the time she got second place in her category.

When I explained the plan to Dasha, she said, "Who?"

"Geraldine," I said. "The Saint Bernard in twenty-two."

"Oh her, yes. She says I'm beautiful," Dasha said.

Dasha was like a foxtail in your ear. All she could talk about was Dasha. I was about to go on a rant about how the whole world didn't revolve around her, when Mouse whapped me

137

with his tail. He bugged his eyes out at me and
I held my bark.

Instead, I said, "Of course she did. We all
do."

It was true. Dasha was stunning. No one
could figure out why she hadn't been adopted.
Even so, there's nothing more difficult than
giving a dog a sincere compliment when you
want to take a bite out of her leg.

"Does she?" Dasha asked.

Mouse's tail continued to hit my leg, so I

nodded. "If there was a Best of Dogtown, you'd win," I said.

Dasha's ears perked up. "You think so?"

"I do," I said.

"Is there a Best of Dogtown trophy?" she asked. She was in her dog show stance. Back straight, ears perked, tail straight out.

Mouse wrapped his tail around my leg and pulled it so tightly it squeezed the blood out of my only front paw. "Not yet," I said.

"Oh," she said.

"So, what about tomorrow?" I asked.

"Tomorrow, yes. You know I've noticed the hair on my hind legs could use a trim. I should get that taken care of before the Best of Dogtown competition," Dasha said, licking her back leg.

"Thank you for helping out Geraldine," I managed to say before Mouse's tail yanked me out of there.

chapter 53

A Lovefest

By the time we opened the next day, everyone had agreed to the tail-out. Now we just needed one human to fall in love with Geraldine.

The first family who came in was only interested in e-dogs. Since the robot dogs had not been charged, the family decided to come back another day.

Next a big, lumbering man with muscular arms bulging out of a black leather vest strode in. He had a scar on his lip and a nose that looked like it had been broken a few times. He was drinking a soda, and when he was done, he crushed the can into a tiny ball in his fist.

But when he saw Bear, curled up sleeping, the man's scary face melted, and I saw the little boy he had once been. "Why hello little one." He clapped his hands, his scarred face as gentle as could be.

When Bear didn't respond, the man's massive shoulders slumped and his eyes got watery.

At Dasha's pen, the big man whistled. "What a beauty."

Dasha being Dasha could not resist a compliment. At first, she preened for him, then remembered what she'd promised and turned tail out. The big man waited for her to turn around. When she didn't, he moved on, the chains around his massive boots clinking with every step.

Trooper, who still had on his Reading Buddy sweater, was doing very well ignoring the man. "Here boy." The man wiggled his big hand into the pocket of his black leather pants and pulled out a dog biscuit.

Trooper's nose twitched; drool dripped from his mouth.

"Come on, fella, I'm not going to hurt you," the man said.

Trooper stared at the biscuit, transfixed.

Then his eyes moved to Geraldine, and he set his chin down in his pool of drool and did not get up.

The man's face grew long, his steps slow, his great shoulders sagged. I was worried he was going to leave before he even got to Geraldine, but he kept walking.

Oh, how he smiled when he saw her, his eyes shining with kindness. "Why hello Geraldine," he said, reading the whiteboard sign.

A volunteer brought Geraldine out and she wagged her tail and nuzzled him. "Aren't you a sweetheart," he said, petting her. He watched her do her tricks. He scratched behind her ear and under her chin, and gave her a belly rub.

It was a lovefest. He was there for the better part of an hour.

Geraldine had found a home.

chapter 54
The Motorcycle

Then, suddenly, I heard the sound of a motor-cycle starting up.

Uh-oh! You couldn't take Geraldine home on a motorcycle. She simply wouldn't fit.

Maybe he had a car at home. Maybe he had a friend with a car. Maybe he would come back wearing hiking boots and walk her home.

But as two o'clock became three and then four, my stomach began to hurt.

If he came back tomorrow, it would be too late.

chapter 55

"When I Was a Kid"

B y this time, the dogs were getting antsy.

They'd given up their chances for a home, and it hadn't helped Geraldine. They were ready to abandon the plan.

I didn't blame them. But, I wasn't going to give up on Geraldine. We had to at least give her one entire day.

As the minutes ticked by, I did what I could to hold the coalition together. The clock said 4:15. A rush of humans came in and then left.

4:30. 4:35. 4:45.

Border collies are good with numbers. Some of us can even tell time. And I have a lot of border collie in me. But on that day, I wished I didn't know what the numbers meant.

Dogtown closed at 5:00. Even if someone wanted Geraldine, there'd be no time to get the paperwork done.

I sat down next to her, wondering what to say. Geraldine spoke first.

"You got a big old heart, Chance," she whispered in her deep voice, her big black nose near my ear. "You gave this your all, dog. First thing I do when I get to doggy heaven, I'm going to snag one of them cloud beds for me and the other I'll save for you. We'll see each other again, dog. You bet we will."

I tried to breathe, but the air wouldn't go in and it wouldn't go out. I had so many feelings

147

welled up in my chest I almost didn't hear the commotion by the front desk.

It sounded like more folks had arrived. I hopped over to check it out.

"I'm sorry, we're about to close," Front Desk announced.

And the people turned around.

It was all I could do to keep from nipping Front Desk's ankles. Didn't she realize this was Geraldine's last day?

And then suddenly a tiny woman in a baseball cap came through the door. She had a great mass of curly gray hair and a big smile set into soft, wrinkled cheeks. By her side was a small boy with a half-hop to his step.

"I'm sorry." Front Desk hurried to the door. "We're about to—"

"We won't be long," the grandma said, plowing by Front Desk.

I liked this little lady's attitude. Grandma types generally head for the small dog pens. But not this one. She and the boy walked by the poodles and Pomeranians as if they didn't exist. And then passed the medium-size dogs: the bulldogs and the beagles.

They walked by all of them, until they got to Geraldine.

Geraldine was tired. She'd done her adopt-me routine more times than we could count that day. I could hear her knees creak when she stood up.

The grandma opened Geraldine's pen door and when she leaned down to pet Geraldine, I couldn't tell whose knees were groaning: the woman's or Geraldine's.

Then the tiny lady said the words that every dog in Dogtown knew were magic. "I had a Saint Bernard when I was a kid. Best dog I ever had."

chapter 56
Last Minutes

There wasn't time for Geraldine to do her routine, so she gave the little boy a big sloppy lick and nuzzled his leg. Then she leaned ever so gently against the gray-haired lady.

Soon Front Desk was on the scene. "I'm sorry, ma'am, Dogtown is closed," she said.

"This is the dog we want. This Geraldine," the grandma declared, as if she hadn't heard a word Front Desk had said.

The little boy gave an oversize nod. Then, he

buried his face in Geraldine's thick fur.

"We're not leaving unless she comes with us," the grandma declared.

Front Desk's eyebrows shot up. Her jaw turned hard, and her hands flew to her hips. "Excuse me, ma'am . . ."

The tiny woman, who was twice the age of Front Desk, strode closer and closer, until she was right up in Front Desk's face. "This dog needs a home," she said.

Front Desk stepped back. She was no match for this woman, who could have been a bouncer, that's how tough she was.

What was Front Desk going to do? Call the police on a tiny gray-haired woman who wanted to give a home to a dog in the last minutes of her last day on Earth?

Front Desk came to her senses. Soon she was bent over the paperwork, and I was saying

151

goodbye to our beloved Geraldine.

"Oh, Chance, you hold it together now, dog. I found me a home," Geraldine whispered, "and you will, too."

Then all of us at Dogtown began to howl as we watched Geraldine lumber out of Dogtown with her forever family.

chapter 57

Group Wag

We celebrated big-time that night. We danced and pranced and staged a Group Wag the likes of which had never been seen. Long and lovely, short and stubby, bushy and bobbed, curly and corkscrew, every dog in Dogtown wagged her tail at the same time.

Our hearts were bursting. We'd done our part to help our sweet Geraldine find her forever home.

"Your heart is a muscle," I told Mouse at dinner that night. "It grows stronger the more you use it."

Metal Head stuck his nose through the fence.

"I'm planning on leaving tomorrow," he announced.

He didn't care to discuss matters of the heart. He was just concerned that I would keep up my end of the deal.

"I'll bring the leash first thing in the morning," I said.

chapter
58
Escape

I always make good on my promises. That may be my Aussie side. We're very responsible.

So, I got up with the first train whistle, hopped behind the counter, picked out a tiny dog leash, and made my way down to the basement.

When I arrived, Mouse was waiting.

"Where are you going?" I asked Metal Head as I pushed the leash through the chain-link.

"Home," he said.

Mouse slipped the handle over his shoulder and began climbing up to the latch.

"How are you planning to get out of Dogtown?"

"I thought you and the little guy would create a distraction. Then I'll sneak out the front door."

I hadn't planned on helping Metal Head with anything beyond getting out of the basement. And I certainly wasn't going to put Mouse in jeopardy. He was more vulnerable than we were. If a human saw him, they'd set a mouse trap, put out poison, or call in the cats.

I shook my head. "Too risky."

"Front Desk likes you. Just go lick her foot," Metal Head suggested as Mouse hooked the leash on the latch and dropped the length down. Metal Head grabbed the leash with his steel teeth and pulled. The latch clicked open, and Metal Head was out.

chapter
59
The Smell of Home

The escape from the basement seemed to happen more quickly than Metal Head thought it would. He quivered as he walked out of his cage.

Was he scared?

Not possible. Metal dogs didn't have feelings of any kind.

Anyhoo, we'd done our part. Now we needed to bow out gracefully.

But it was still early. Front Desk and the

volunteers didn't come until 7:30. So we walked with Metal Head to the lobby. No danger in that.

Then Metal Head did something that surprised me. He started talking about his human.

"I find great satisfaction in hearing my little human, Jimmy, read to me. I love when he talks about his adventures at school. Once he brought me to show-and-tell, and all the kids took turns giving me orders. Oh, what a day that was!"

I love stories, so I stayed a little longer than I should have. The next thing I knew there were footsteps on the path.

We ducked behind the counter. The keys clinked; the lock turned.

"Awful stuffy in here," Management told a volunteer as she pushed open the door.

"At least it's warm," the volunteer said, taking her mittens off.

"I'm going to keep the door open for just a minute to air the place out," Management said, propping open the door with a bag of kibble.

The smells coming from outdoors flooded my nostrils.

Wet leaves. Pine trees. Wood fires burning. The intense aroma of blue sky.

I hadn't smelled the outside in such a long time.

When Management and the volunteer had gone to put their lunches away, I hopped to the door. Just close enough to get a nose full of freedom.

What was the harm in one little sniff?

chapter 60
The Call of the Open Door

We waited for Management and the volunteer to walk back to the employee break room to put their lunches in the refrigerator.

Now with the door propped open, all Metal Head would have to do was walk out.

Mouse climbed on my back, and we escorted Metal Head to the door. "Good luck," I said.

But the smell . . . I couldn't turn away. Even the best trained dogs have a difficult time resisting an open door.

Still, I knew better. It was the beginning of December. There was no way a three-legged dog and a small mouse could survive the winter outside.

I turned away from the open door. But as I did, I saw something.

Something I had dreamed about every night.

chapter 61

The Sign

I saw a sign with a dog's photo and the words: LOST DOG.

I have trouble deciphering photos sometimes, especially from a distance. But the dog in the photo had a white patch over her eye.

The dog's paws were tucked under her so I couldn't tell if there were three or four. But the Bessers wouldn't know I had three legs. All of their photos of me would be from back when I had four legs.

Of course, I knew I'd been gone for nearly a year. The chances of there being a sign for me were infinitesimal. But there it was!

Management had said Dogtown needed airing out. The door would be open for a little while anyway. I would hop to the sign, see who was on it, and hop back inside.

Easy peasy.

Mouse thought this was a bad idea. His tail was whapping me on my left side, then on my right.

But I ignored him, like I was in a trance.

Jessie and Professor Besser were looking for me!

chapter 62

Lost Dog

I hobbled as fast as I could to the telephone pole, with Mouse grasping my fur and whapping me with his tail.

My heart began to pound. I could almost smell the blueberry pancakes. The closer I got, the slower I hopped. The dog had a patch over his eye just like me, but his hair was shorter and his nose not so pointy.

I just needed to see it better I told myself.

But when I got closer, it didn't say *Lost Dog*.
It said *Last Blog*.

It was a dog blog. The last one of the year.
And the dog in the photo was not me.

Forever Home

In my mind, I was back under the Bessers' table curled up at Jessie's feet while she did her homework. I could smell the salmon as it came out of the oven. I could hear the fish scraps hit my bowl, and I could feel the warmth of Jessie's toes under my cheek.

But now here I was on the cold, hard ground. My nose running. My paws freezing. The cold wind ruffling my fur.

I wasn't even embarrassed that I had acted

like a first day boohoo in front of Mouse and Metal Head. I was just sad.

I suspected my mistake had something to do with Geraldine. I'd trusted her and when she'd said I'd find my forever home, I believed her.

She gave me hope. And hope is a painful business.

chapter 64
The Closed Door

Sorry, Mouse," I said as I began hopping back to Dogtown.

The door was still open. If I hurried, we could slip back inside before anyone saw us.

"Wait!" Metal Head called.

Metal Head wanted us to go with him. Who wouldn't prefer to travel with company?

But I knew I had to look after Mouse and me. Even if by some crazy miracle Metal Head's humans wanted him back, they certainly wouldn't want a tiny rodent and a three-legged dog.

"Look!" Metal Head shouted.

Front Desk was walking up the path. I ducked behind a bush. When I peeked out, she'd locked the door. The shelter wasn't open to the public until ten o'clock.

Management would come back. She'd open the door to air out the place, wouldn't she?

But Management didn't come back.

The door stayed closed.

171

chapter 65

Last Chance

It's only a few hours. Why not enjoy your freedom for a little while? You can always go back. Why not take a chance?" Metal Head asked.

I never liked it when dogs used my name against me. *It's your last chance. It's your only chance. Take a chance. Give me a chance.*

So annoying.

Anyhoo, I wasn't about to go with Metal Head. "I'll slow you down," I said.

"It's not that far. No stairs or hills. It's no

MISSING:

Best DOG a Jessie
could ever want.
Answers to "CHANCE"
Loves Professor,
Ear rubs, eating
blueberry Pancakes,
and company of a
MOUSE.

farther than three round trips to the basement. You'll have to wait until Dogtown opens to return, anyway. Why not have a little adventure?"

I shook my head.

"Don't you want to see my home?" Metal Head pleaded.

I did, actually.

I can't say that Metal Head was a friend, then. He was more of a friend of a friend. Quinn liked him and I liked Quinn.

But yeah, I did want to see if everything worked out for him. But that wasn't the real reason I said yes.

The real reason was something I didn't want to admit . . .

There were a lot of phone poles up ahead. And maybe they had signs, too.

chapter 66

A Discussion with Mouse

Mouse wasn't happy with me. He didn't like it when I took matters into my own paws without consulting him.

He looked me in the eyes and gave me a real talking-to with his busy little hands.

There's nothing like getting bawled out by a three-inch mouse.

Mouse kept pointing to his wrist, which meant we needed to be back by suppertime. He had mouths to feed.

I had to be back, too. It was Wednesday. Poker night.

Mouse seesawed his head.

"We'll be back before lunch," I said. "We'll wait for Front Desk to go to the restroom, and then we'll duck back inside."

No one would miss me. Dogtown was a pretty big place and I was always moving around.

Mouse nodded. He didn't look happy about the plan, but he agreed.

Metal Head just sat there, watching. When I told him we were coming along, his tail began to wag, something I had not seen before.

chapter 67

Why We Steal Socks

Metal Head couldn't wait to get home. But he was kind about letting me stop and rest when I needed to.

He'd been right, though. I was in good shape from all the trips up and down the basement stairs. It was the telephone poles that slowed me down.

Sometimes it was a poster for a play or an ad for perfume. (I will never understand perfume. Why would you want to cover up your hind end smell? Humans don't understand why we steal their underwear and socks. But how do you know a person if you don't smell their feet?)

Mostly, though, the posters were for lost pets. I saw flyers for two cats and a dog. The dog had been in Dogtown when I first got there. His humans had found him and brought him back home.

See, that was the other thing I didn't like to think about. If you were missing your dog, wouldn't you call Dogtown to see if your dog was there?

I'd heard Management field calls like that. There were lots of them.

chapter
68

Puppy Love

Of course, we weren't the only shelter in town. There was South City and Pet Rescue.

Maybe my humans had called those places.

Or maybe they didn't post a sign because they didn't have a staple gun. More likely they had a new dog—a puppy with four legs. He was probably sleeping in my bed, eating from my bowl, and getting petted by my people.

Thoughts like these stung. I wished I could stop myself from thinking them.

chapter
69
The House on Spring Valley Road

The trip went quickly. The second I'd get tired I'd see another telephone pole and that would get me going again.

Metal Head was so confident that I began to wonder if the situation with robot dogs might be different. You didn't have to feed a metal dog, fill his water bowl, or take him on walks. If you got tired of him, you could shove him in the closet. I'd heard Management talking about how hard it was to find old robot dogs when she started Dogtown 2.0.

On the other hand, closets got full, didn't they? And somebody had given up Metal Head, hadn't they?

Anyhoo, I stopped worrying about Metal Head. Clearly he knew more than I did about the lifespan of a metal dog.

After a while, Metal Head began to prance on his clunky metal paws.

He was so excited his tail was sticking straight up in the air. We were getting close to a yellow house with a white picket fence and a wraparound porch. It had a lovely evergreen tree and a small yellow playhouse with white trim just like the real house.

22 Spring Valley Road was the kind of home a dog only dreamed about. And I was about to tell him that when he said, "I have a gift for you. A token of my appreciation for your help." He had something for us! My mind filled with visions of bacon glistening with grease, buffalo burgers, and butter-basted beef.

"We'll go in through the garage," he said. "June leaves for school at 8:30 and the garage door will open."

That worried me. Why wouldn't he go in the front door?

But then I thought about the gift, which might be table scraps. I would do anything for table scraps. What dog wouldn't?

chapter 70

The Garage Door

At 8:30 the garage door opened just like Metal Head said it would, and the car shot backward onto the driveway and into the street. The driver, a teenage girl with blue hair, shifted to drive, then ripped up the road without looking back.

If she had glanced in the rearview mirror, she'd have seen a three-legged dog, a metal pooch, and a mouse steal into the garage before the door closed with a clunk.

I jumped at the sound. We were locked in!

Metal Head must have seen the expression on my face, because he pointed to a button that operated the garage door. "That's how you open the door. Mouse can climb up, should that be required. Now, I thought you might enjoy some cheese."

Cheese!

He instructed Mouse to hook a small rope through the handle of a refrigerator. Then he pulled it open and rummaged around in there before producing a plate with two cheese sandwiches. A big one for me and a little one for Mouse.

The smell of cheese is simply divine. The taste of it is even better.

It was almost worth the trip just for that.

chapter 71

The Warm Kitchen

Tasting that cheese brought back the Bessers' warm kitchen. The smell of freshly baked Parmesan bread. The salty snap of salami and cheese. The fluffy softness of a cheese soufflé. There was always a treat in my bowl.

And Jessie and Professor Besser were always there to wrap me in a blanket when it was cold. Take me swimming when it was hot. Dry my paws when it rained. And pull foxtails from my fur after a walk in the woods.

How safe I had felt with them.

chapter 72
The Cheese Helped

W hen you're finished, you can let yourself out," said Metal Head. "The garage door often misfires for no apparent reason. No one will think it unusual if it opens now."

I felt a certain fondness for Metal Head right then. He'd given us a gift.

(In case you were wondering what to give a dog and a mouse . . . a cheese sandwich is it.)

Then, we all said our goodbyes.

I was still biased against metal dogs at that

point. But I was opening my mind to the possibility that a bond between a real dog and a robot dog might be possible. I had come to respect Metal Head. Maybe even like him.

The cheese helped, okay? It did.

73

Jimmy

We watched as Metal Head went in the house through a door at the front of the garage.

He was sure of himself. And why shouldn't he be? Everything he'd said had turned out to be true.

We were just packing up the rest of the cheese sandwiches when we heard a teenage boy shout, "What is that stupid dog toy doing here? I thought you gave him away."

"What dog? Oh. Yeah. We did give him away.

Months ago," a lady answered. "Your dad took him to the shelter."

"Why's he back?"

"I have no idea."

"Well can you please take him? Ben is coming over after school. And he might bring Derek. *Derek!* I can't have a toy dog following me around like I'm five."

"I know, Sweetie."

"Mom! My name is James. Not Sweetie, Jimmy Poo, or Jammy face. James! Do you understand?"

"Right. James. I'm sorry."

"Here. Take him."

"Okay, okay. I've got a donation box in my trunk. I'll take him this afternoon."

In her trunk? Uh-oh! Mouse and I dove behind the recycling bin.

"Oh, how you loved that dog!" Mom said. "Don't

you remember how you'd read to him for hours?"

"Mom, hello? I'm in middle school!"

"I know, James. I got it."

"Turn him off. Otherwise, he'll find me."

"He'll find you?" Mom laughed.

"Don't make fun of me!" James shouted.

"I'm not making fun of you. But he's not going to find you. He's just a toy. Now eat your breakfast. You'll be late for school."

We heard footsteps in the garage. I peeked out and saw a woman with a ponytail and squeaky yellow sneakers come through the door carrying Metal Head. She turned him over and flipped his off switch. Then she reached through the open driver's side window and clicked a button. The trunk popped open, and she placed Metal Head inside.

Then she closed the trunk with a *whomp* and walked away.

chapter 74

Part of Our Pack

The garage and the house were quiet. Evidently, James had finished his breakfast and gone to school. The car was still in the garage, and there was no sign of Mom.

I considered hightailing it out of there. But I couldn't abandon Metal Head, especially since Mom had turned him off.

I could never leave a dog defenseless like that.

Even if he was made of metal, he was part of our pack.

One look at Mouse and I knew he felt the same way.

chapter 75

The Dashboard

The first order of business was getting Metal Head out. Mom had reached through the window and pushed a button that released the trunk. But which button?

I'd been in the Bessers' car a hundred times before, but who noticed the location of the trunk release? Besides, their car was different from this one.

Even so, I knew more than Mouse who had never been in a car before. Mouse climbed up the tire and tried to get a grip on the slippery metal of the door. He wedged his toes in the door crack and held on with flat palms. Slowly he worked his way up to the handle. From there, he dove in the open window.

Once he was in, I began explaining the dashboard.

"Each button and dial operates something, but I don't exactly know what. You'll have to experiment."

Mouse started pushing buttons, twisting dials, and flipping switches. Nothing happened.

Then suddenly the windshield wipers started up and the lights went on. Then the horn blared.

"Hide! Quick!" I shouted, diving behind the recycling bin.

We waited a long time, but it was quiet. No one had heard us, so Mouse, who had slipped

into the inside door pocket, climbed out and began pushing buttons again. Then bingo, the trunk popped open.

But just as it did Mom flung the door to the garage open and peeked out.

I dove behind the tire and held my breath.

Mom trotted over to the car and turned the lights and the windshield wipers off. "Very funny, James," she called out. "Now please go to school. I don't want to get another email that says: *Your child has been tardy.*"

She went around the back, slammed the trunk closed, and stomped into the house.

chapter 76

The Trunk

We waited and waited until we were sure she was not coming back.

Then, Mouse popped the trunk again, crawled out the window, hopped onto the door handle, and slid the rest of the way down. I jumped up, resting my one front paw on the bumper, and peered inside. The trunk was a tornado of tents, tarps, tennis rackets, and teddy bears.

And there, in the middle of the mess, was

a box marked DONATION, with Metal Head's hind end sticking out. Mouse scrambled up my leg, to my back, then up my neck to my head. From there, he leapt into the trunk and dug around until he found Metal Head's switch. He flipped it on, and Metal Head's lights flashed blue, then yellow.

"Metal Head," I barked.

He didn't answer.

Didn't move.

Didn't say a word.

Had he been damaged by the toss into the donation box?

"Hey, Metal Head, hello?" I said.

Still nothing except his lights flickering blue and yellow.

chapter 77

E-Waste

I doubted I could jump into the trunk. Don't get me wrong, if I was in a three-legged race, I'd win, paws down. My back legs are strong. And that's what propels a leap like that.

But there wasn't room in the garage for me to get a running start. I would have to pull myself up by one leg.

I squirmed up, then slid back down. Then I tried again, pushing off with my back legs, twisting myself forward. It wasn't pretty, but

I somehow managed to wiggle into the trunk.

I was panting hard as I crawled through the trunk junk to Metal Head.

Mouse was there already. He was waving his arms all around trying to get Metal Head's attention.

"Hey, buddy." I looked Metal Head in the eye. Mouse tapped him on the ear. "You don't want to be donated," I said. "They'll put you in e-waste."

He didn't answer, but his eyelids flickered. Robot dogs were afraid of e-waste. Nobody wants to be recycled.

And then suddenly I understood what was going on.

Metal Head had a heart. And it was broken.

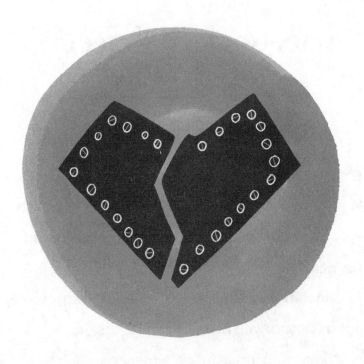

chapter 78

The Boohoo Speech

At least I knew what to do about a dog with a broken heart. I launched into my boohoo speech, which I had pretty much perfected after nearly a year in Dogtown.

"Just because a human doesn't want you, doesn't mean you aren't lovable," I said.

"Save your breath," he whispered.

So, he could talk. That was good.

"You have to get out of here, Metal Head."

Mouse nodded vigorously. He pointed to the garage door.

"Just turn me off," Metal Head said.

"You'll get over this. I've had my heart broken and I survived. You will, too."

"Jimmy and I did everything together." His voice broke.

THE MAGIC #

"Yeah, but Jimmy's growing up."

"Why would you upgrade when the kid model is flawless?" Metal Head asked.

"I don't know," I said, thinking how perfect my Jessie was.

"It hurts"—he tapped his chest—"right here."

"That's your heart," I said.

"What is the point of having one? It's an inferior design," Metal Head said.

"Love is complicated," I explained. "Your boy loves you. But right now, he's trying so hard to grow up, he has to pretend he doesn't."

Metal Head nodded miserably. "I embarrass him. He called me a toy."

"I'm sorry."

"You're always telling dogs to get over their boohoos. You have no real understanding of what it feels like."

I swallowed past a knot in my throat. "That's not true," I said.

I didn't want to tell him my story, especially with Mouse jabbing my sides with his tiny finger. Mouse wanted us out of there. Any second Jimmy's mom could come out and drive us away. I saw his point, but what could I do? Metal Head wasn't going to budge until I made him understand that he would have a life after Jimmy.

So, I took a deep breath and began.

chapter
79

Back When I Had Four Legs

My life was wonderful back when I had four legs and I lived with Jessie and Professor Besser. I didn't know there were dogs in the world who weren't loved like I was. I'd never even heard of a dog shelter. A bad day back then was no dogs at the dog park.

I went right from the tender paws of my mama to the Bessers' home on Sycamore Avenue. Jessie was six then and had wanted a dog her whole life. She was overjoyed from the first moment she saw me. She dressed me in dolly outfits. She shared her snacks with me. And she let me hide my bones under her pillow.

When Jessie went to school, I'd wait by the door until she came home. I'd get so excited when I heard the squeak of the bus brakes, the slap of the bus door, and Jessie's feet skipping down the steps.

Jessie threw the ball for me. We played Milk-Bone hide-and-seek and watched our favorite TV programs cuddled together on the couch. We never grew tired of playing with each other.

Jessie smelled of pencils and baby powder and blueberry pancakes, which is the best smell in the entire world.

80

Sabbatical

One day I learned a new word.

Sabbatical.

A sabbatical is six months of paid leave. I figured that meant Professor Besser wouldn't have to go to work for six whole months. It was a dream come true. She'd be home all day with me.

Until Jessie began to ask questions.

"Why do I have to learn Italian?"

"Why do I have to go to a new school?"

"When are we leaving?"

"Why can't Chance come with us?"

chapter

81

Open Suitcase

Then the suitcases came out.

I had some good friends in the neighborhood, two Labs named Harry and Jerry. Harry and Jerry had warned me of the dangers of an open suitcase.

Suitcases meant your humans were leaving. If you were lucky, you would go with them. And if you weren't . . .

"Watch to see if they pack your food and your leash," Harry had said.

"If they don't," Jerry yipped, "you're in trouble."

Every day I watched.

And every day the leash embroidered with my name stayed in the hall closet.

I told myself that Harry and Jerry were just trying to scare me with their suitcase talk.

But I had a bad feeling about it.

Finally, the day came when the suitcases were zippered closed. Then, a young lady with a pink nose and a sharp chin rang the front bell.

She smelled of chlorine and cherry cough syrup. Never trust a human who smells like that.

But Professor Besser had weak olfactory glands. All humans do. Without a good nose, they have no idea who to trust.

chapter 82

The Dog-Sitter

It all happened so fast.

Professor Besser and Jessie wheeled their suitcases out the door. Jessie sobbed while the lady they called "the house-sitter" or sometimes "the dog-sitter" held my collar.

"Don't worry, I'll take good care of Chance." She patted my head like she was dribbling a basketball. When I tried leaning against her leg, she leapt away as if I had fleas.

I whimpered. I barked. I wiggled out of the dog-sitter's grasp and took off.

I had four legs back then, so I ran fast. But not fast enough. The door shut in my face. I stared out the window as Jessie and Professor Besser drove away.

chapter
83
The Dog-Sitter's Boyfriend

I dislike the term *dog-sitter*. Dogs are not chairs. We are not couches. We are not tables.

Maybe if I'd had a kind dog-sitter, I wouldn't hate the word so much.

But I did not. By lunchtime on the first day, my water bowl had dried up and I was forced to drink from the toilet. Something no dignified dog ever does.

Then my kibble bowl went empty. The

dog-sitter refilled it occasionally, but not often and never with table scraps.

Then the smells of my home began to change.

The blueberry pancake smell?

Gone.

The toasted almonds smell?

Gone.

The manila folder smell?

Gone.

Now the place reeked of chlorine, cherry cough syrup, bleach, burnt plastic, and bad breath.

Only the yard smelled the same. Like pine and sycamore trees and squirrel nuts and Harry and Jerry's pee—and mine, too, of course.

And if that weren't bad enough, the boy-friend arrived.

The dog-sitter's boyfriend didn't care for me.

And as far as I could tell, he didn't care for the dog-sitter, either.

Humans are confusing. No dog would stay with a mate who treated her badly. Sure, we have our share of bossy dogs. But leadership is one thing. Mistreatment is another.

I couldn't stand either of them. I spent as much time as possible in the yard, but we had a rough winter and the weather was bitter cold.

Icy rain, hail, snow, and a biting wind. The weather forced the dog-sitter and the dog-sitter's boyfriend indoors. The house on Sycamore Avenue, which had been so cozy with the Bessers, grew smaller and smaller with the dog-sitter and the dog-sitter's boyfriend locked inside.

I did my best to stay out of their way.

chapter 84
For the Love of Salami

Then one night, the dog-sitter and the dog-sitter's boyfriend had a terrible fight. The boyfriend said mean things I'm not going to repeat. The dog-sitter hurled a salami against the wall.

The boyfriend stomped out, got in his truck, and careened down the driveway.

The dog-sitter retreated to the bedroom. I tiptoed on silent paws to retrieve the salami, which had rolled under the couch.

I knew it was risky, but the smell of salami was too tempting.

The dog-sitter must have heard me, because she tore out of the bedroom and lunged for my collar. "That's mine," she shouted, grabbing the salami and shoving me out into the cold, dark night.

I huddled outside, shivering, my paws like ice cubes. Soon I began whining at the door.

"SHUT UP!" the dog-sitter shouted.

I hid under a bush. It was covered in snow, but the ground underneath was dry.

The boyfriend's truck roared back into the driveway and the boyfriend hopped out, leaving the truck running.

He'd forgotten his coat. He came out of the house a minute later, all bundled up in his puffy coat, big leather gloves, and knit cap.

I decided that huddling near the door on the back porch might be warmer. So, I made a dash from the bush to the back porch. The route I took was nowhere near the truck.

But the driveway was icy and the truck spun out of control.

When I woke up, I had three legs.

chapter 85
"It's the Dog's Fault"

The dog-sitter and her boyfriend took me to the vet, at least. When I came back all bandaged up, I heard them talking.

"I can't tell the Bessers we ran over her leg. How will that look?" the dog-sitter asked.

"Yeah, they might not pay you. Tell them the dog ran away."

"Why is that better?"

"Because then it's the dog's fault," said the boyfriend. "Not yours."

"How are we going to pay the vet bill?"

"Dog food money. We won't need to feed her anymore. She'll be gone."

"Good idea!" said the dog-sitter, planting a kiss on her boyfriend's cheek.

That's when I knew I had to run away. My life depended on it.

chapter 86
Back of the Truck

I was new to the three-legged business. I moved even slower than I do now. And I got very tired.

I hadn't even made it to the mailbox by the time the boyfriend found me. He grabbed me, ripped my dog tags off, and tossed me in the back of his truck. Then he climbed in the cab and the truck shot forward.

I knew wherever he was taking me, I didn't want to go. But the dog-sitter's boyfriend was stronger than I was and weighed five times as much. My only hope was to jump out. At the first stoplight, there were cars on either side. Even if I managed to jump out of the truck, I didn't see how I could avoid being run over. Then we got on the freeway and there was nothing I could do.

When we finally got off, I was ready. At the first stop sign, I hooked one paw over the side of the truck and shoved off with my back legs. I landed upside down in a snow drift. When I dug myself out the dog-sitter's boyfriend was gone.

I had no idea where to go. But as cold and scared as I was, it was still better than being home with the dog-sitter and the dog-sitter's boyfriend.

The boyfriend's last words had been chilling. "We won't need to feed her anymore. She'll be gone."

chapter 87

The Smell of Walnuts and Honey

I did what any dog would do . . . I followed my nose.

I stayed away from scary smells like cigarette smoke and spoiled meat. And I hopped toward good smells like dumplings and deviled eggs.

My nose led me to a restaurant that smelled of beef and broccoli and orange chicken. I curled up near the door, which was warm from the restaurant kitchen, and slept. When I woke up, a man with kind eyes and gentle hands was kneeling down next to me. He smelled of walnuts and honey.

"Poor thing," he said, "you come with me." I followed him to his car. He turned on the heater and soon it was warm and toasty. I nuzzled his leg.

He checked my collar. There were no tags. The dog-sitter's boyfriend had made sure of that. But my name was embroidered on my collar.

"What a love you are, Chance. I wish I could take you home with me, doggy," he said. "But my landlord won't let me have pets."

He took a long time petting me, like he really didn't want to stop. And then he clicked on his seat belt and drove me to Dogtown.

We arrived just before closing. Front Desk was locking up. "I found her outside our restaurant. She's a sweetheart." He set me down at Front Desk's feet. "You'll take good care of her?"

"We'll do our best," said Front Desk.

He gave me one last pat, then turned and walked away.

chapter
88
Wondering

I knew the dog-sitter and her boyfriend wouldn't be looking for me. But every day I wondered if Jessie and Professor Besser would come back from their sabbatical and search for me.

Day after day, week after week, month after month, they didn't come, and my heart broke all over again.

After a while it was too painful to wonder anymore.

chapter
89
"No!"

ow do you believe I know how you feel?" I
asked Metal Head.

Metal Head nodded. Mouse did too. He knew
most of the story already. Even so, he pulled a
piece of toilet paper off the roll in the trunk and
dabbed at his face.

"So come with us," I said.

"No!" Metal Head said, closing his eyes.

chapter
90
The Mind of a Metal Dog

I didn't know what else to say. I'd always been successful getting boohoos to move on. And that was without telling them my own boohoo story.

I'd pulled out all the stops with Metal Head and it had made no difference at all.

Maybe he couldn't relate to a *real* dog's story. Or maybe, once a robot dog's mind was made up, he couldn't change it. Metal is not a flexible material.

I was considering my next steps when Mouse tapped my leg and motioned for me to follow him.

There wasn't much room in the trunk, packed as it was. I climbed over a yoga mat and some hockey sticks to where Mouse was digging in the donation box. He pulled up the hard corner of something.

I thought maybe it was a manual. Something to help us understand our metal friend.

But it wasn't a manual. It was *Green Eggs and Ham*.

chapter 91

Reading Buddy

I dragged the book to Metal Head.

"Metal Head! Look! It was in the donation box. Jimmy's done with it. We can take it to Quinn."

"Quinn was suspended," he said.

"Right . . . but you know what *suspended* means."

"Temporary removal of a student," he said in his drone voice.

"Yeah, *temporary*. You know how excited

Quinn was when you read to him. He'll be back."

Metal Head nodded. His expression hadn't changed, but his blue lights began to flash brighter.

I leaned in. "What if he returns to Reading Buddies and his book still isn't there? He might throw a fit. Do you want him to get suspended again?"

Metal Head shook his head, a tiny motion, more like a tremor than a shake.

"You have to bring the book back to Quinn."

"You can deliver it," he said.

"But I can't read *Green Eggs and Ham* to Quinn. He doesn't understand Dog. You're his Reading Buddy. He doesn't want anyone else."

"I want to be home with Jimmy."

This was a tough one. What could I say to that?

I thought for a long time before I opened my mouth. "You did your job. You helped Jimmy grow up."

I paused, letting this sink in. "It's Quinn who needs you now."

chapter
92

Flashing Lights

Metal Head wasn't totally convinced. But all his lights were flashing extra bright. The blue, the white, and the bright yellow. I suspected that meant his steel heart was beating again.

It didn't take much more to persuade him to return to Dogtown with us.

He had just climbed out of the donation box when we heard the footsteps.

chapter
93

In the Trunk

Jimmy's mom stomped to the trunk.

I thought for sure she'd notice us. We were right there in plain sight. But she didn't look closely. "I could have sworn I shut this," she said and slammed the trunk shut.

Bang and the world went dark.

94

Thrift Store

A moment later, the motor started up, the garage door opened, and the car rolled out.

We were on our way to the thrift store.

At first, we were terrified. But slowly our eyes adjusted to the dark. There was a faint line of light around the trunk's edge which helped. We found an old tarp and hid beneath it, my paw wrapped around *Green Eggs and Ham*.

Then the errands started. Each time we pulled into a parking space, we held our breath.

But stop after stop, the trunk stayed closed.

Humans and their errands! Makes me glad I'm a dog.

After seven stops hiding under the tarp, the thrift store started to look pretty good. It was afternoon by the time Mom finally popped the lock.

Mouse clutched my leg. This was it!

But no.

Mom grabbed her yoga mat and shut the trunk. A long time later, she put the mat back. By then, it was late afternoon. Had she forgotten about the thrift store?

Once again she started the car. We took a few turns and bumped over some potholes. Then the car stopped, the trunk opened, and she lifted out the donation box.

She struggled to carry the box and close the trunk at the same time but couldn't quite do it, so she left the trunk open.

I peeked out from under the tarp and watched her duck into the thrift store. Metal Head got out first clutching *Green Eggs and Ham*, then Mouse and I hopped out, taking cover under a nearby car.

We were just thinking we'd made it when we heard Mom's squeaky sneakers headed in our direction. She leaned over the trunk and began digging inside.

Had she noticed that Metal Head was not in the box?

She took out the tarp, the yoga mat, the hockey sticks, the toilet paper, and the largest teddy bear. She pawed around for a while before putting everything back.

We heard her make a call on her cell phone.

"Hi, honey, I'm at the thrift store. Strangest

thing happened today. Remember that robot dog toy Jimmy loved so much?"

She paused.

"Uh-huh, yeah. I thought we gave him away, too, but apparently not. And James got all upset when he saw him, so I said I'd take him to the thrift store. I put him in the trunk and now he's gone."

She paused, again. "He *was* a strange toy. Remember we got him from that man at the flea market?

"Right, yeah. Maybe he was in the bottom of the box and I just didn't notice. Or maybe I'm losing it, because I'm telling you this has been the weirdest day!"

Another pause, followed by a laugh. "You're going to get pizza for dinner? See, this is why I married you. Pizza solves everything. Okay, see you at home. Love you, too."

chapter
95
Two Legs

Mom closed the trunk and drove away.

At first, we were happy to be out of there. Then the worries set in.

Mouse and I were hungry and thirsty. And we had no idea how to get back to Dogtown.

I peeked out from under the car. Generally, I have a good sense of direction. But I'd gotten turned around from all the stops. I didn't know if we were fifty yards from Dogtown or fifty miles.

It was going to be dark soon. The day had

been unseasonably warm, but the nights were freezing. This wouldn't be a problem for Metal Head. But I worried about Mouse. His fur wasn't thick like mine.

And after what had happened with the dog-sitter's boyfriend, I was terrified of the city streets at night.

What if I lost another leg? I'd never seen a dog with two legs. Which tells you something, doesn't it?

"I have to get back for poker night," I said, but still, I didn't move. I couldn't decide whether to go left or right.

Metal Head and Mouse nodded. They knew poker night was what kept me off The List.

Then Mouse gestured wildly with his hands. He was worried his brothers and sisters back at Dogtown would go hungry without him. I felt bad about this because Mouse hadn't wanted to come along in the first place.

"My charge is low. Five percent," Metal Head reported.

"Five percent!" I howled.

Mouse dove under Metal Head to check his charging gauge, which was tucked into his belly. Mouse held two fingers up with his left hand and two with his right.

"Twenty-two minutes," I said.

Mouse nodded a big nod.

"We'll have to find a charge on our way home," I said bravely. What else could we do?

chapter 96
Train Whistle

I could smell a hundred things at once. Biscuits, bananas, and burnt coffee, fish that was dried and fish that was fried. We were in a strip mall that included the thrift store, a little grocery, a bakery, a fish market, and a furniture store.

I heard the train whistle. A short toot, then a long one. The sound stretched as the train pulled away.

The evening whistle wasn't as loud here as

it had been at Dogtown. And I couldn't hear the clanking of the railroad crossing arm.

I didn't know how far we'd traveled with Jimmy's mom. Still, it was comforting to hear the familiar sound.

What I needed was a map. But there was no time to think about that. Metal Head's charge was running out.

Fish Market

Metal Head was moving slowly. "How long do you take to charge?" I asked.

"Four hours," he said in his low-charge drawl.

"Four hours!" I began to pant. "You must be joking!"

You can say what you want about a real dog's needs, but at least we don't require an electrical umbilical cord.

What if there was a power outage? Robot dogs would all stop.

Once Metal Head's charge got to zero, his limbs would freeze up. He wouldn't be able to move. And he was much too heavy for Mouse and me to carry.

Mouse scrambled on my back and we headed for the fish market. The smells were

intoxicating. Salmon, sole, steelhead trout . . .
I hadn't had fish since Sycamore Avenue. The
professor liked grilled salmon. There was always a curl of fish skin, a chunk of fish flesh, a
bit of fish fat in my bowl. Jessie had been fond
of tuna melts. Sometimes I got to lick the can.

If we could get a bite of dinner for Mouse
and me and a charge for Metal Head . . . what
could be better than that?

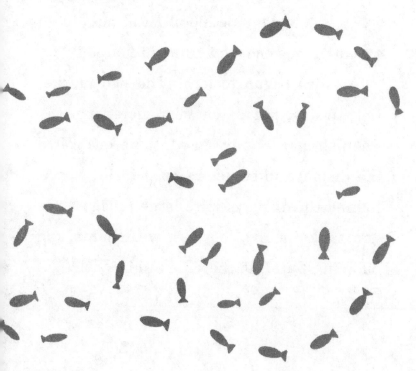

chapter

98

A Risky Move

How would we hide Metal Head next to an outlet long enough for him to charge?

An idea began to form. The fish market was closing, but a few customers lingered. The fish market guys in white aprons rolled the displays into the cramped inside space. Behind the displays were large refrigerators and tanks of live lobsters, with lights and bubbling water, so there had to be outlets in there.

What if the fish market was locked up with us inside? I licked my lips at the thought.

I was thinking how we might stage a distraction and scoot inside without being seen, when Mouse slipped off my back and bolted across the sidewalk.

Mouse!

With all the people around, this was a risky move.

Mouse didn't panic when they spotted him, either. He climbed up a table leg and retrieved a piece of shrimp, which hadn't yet been cleared away.

"Rat! Rat!" a woman in purple tights shouted, waving her walking stick.

By then Mouse was running back across the sidewalk, the shrimp in his mouth, a guy with a broom chasing after him.

chapter 99

The Broom

I knew better than to run. And Metal Head, low as he was on charge, could barely walk.

So the two of us sat outside pretending to be loyal canines waiting for our humans to come out of the market.

Mouse disappeared under a parked car.

The fish market guy who had a ponytail and smelled like lemons, circled the car, broom in hand. He thumped the bristles on the cement.

He peered underneath and ran the broom under the car.

Still no Mouse.

The fish market guy stood up and smacked the broom handle on the pavement. It made a terrifying *CRACK* and Mouse darted out.

The fish market guy took off after him.

Mouse headed for the bakery. He bypassed a car, barely missing a lady carrying a bakery box. But the fish market guy slammed into her, sending the pink bakery box flying.

"Come on!" I barked as the fish market guy apologized to the woman and helped her gather the bags of cookies that had spilled on the pavement.

Mouse scampered onto my back and the three of us hightailed it out of there.

"Mouse!" I growled, when we were a safe distance away. "Are you nuts? You could have gotten killed."

Mouse made a sign for hungry, then hung his head, his glossy black eyes fixated on the sidewalk.

"I know," I said. "I'm hungry, too."

Mouse produced the small piece of shrimp he'd been holding in his mouth. He offered me half, but I didn't take it.

One half of a shrimp scrap would only wake up my stomach. And that was the last thing I needed to do.

chapter 100
The Dog Who Could Read

We were halfway to the grocery store by the time I remembered *Green Eggs and Ham*!

"We forgot the book. I'll go find it. Meet you outside the furniture store."

I hurried back to search behind the dumpster, by the cars, on the sidewalk. I finally found *Green Eggs and Ham* in front of the fish market. I picked it up with my teeth and began hopping back to Metal Head and Mouse.

By now, the market was closed and two of

the market guys were leaving. The guy with the ponytail who had chased Mouse. And a tall guy who reeked of garlic.

"There's that lame dog again," Garlic Breath said.

That raised my hackles. It's true I'm missing a leg, but there's so much more to me than that.

"He was a friend of the stupid mouse that made me run into the lady," Ponytail said.

"He was *a friend* of the mouse?" Garlic Breath snickered.

"Yeah. What's he got in his mouth?" Ponytail asked. "Wait . . . it's a book. I think it's *Green Eggs and Ham*. Remember that one?"

"Let's see . . . a dog who can read has a friend who's a mouse. What'd you eat for lunch, man?" Garlic Breath asked as he got in his car.

Ponytail laughed and I wagged my tail,

because I wasn't just a lame dog to them now. I was a dog who could read and had a mouse as a friend. A book and a friend . . . what could be better than that?

chapter 101

The Furniture Store

When I caught up with Metal Head and Mouse, they were tucked behind an arrangement of pots outside the furniture store. The ights were still on, but the store looked closed.

We went around the back, and found the door propped open. What luck!

I stuck my nose through the doorway and inhaled the aroma of varnish, Styrofoam, and burnt popcorn. It sounded like a television was on. A dance show of some kind. Pounding feet followed the dance beat cadence.

I told Mouse and Metal Head to wait near some bushes. Then I hopped in to check out the situation.

It probably would have been smarter to have Mouse scout things out, because he's so much smaller. But he was still working on his shrimp scrap, and I hated to interrupt his dinner.

The furniture store was even bigger than it had looked from the outside. I saw a room full of couches. Oh, how I love a good couch!

(In case you didn't know, the world is made up of two kinds of humans. Those that allow their dogs on the couch, and those that don't. Professor Besser let me sleep on the couch. Of course she did.)

In the mattress section, I noticed an unused electrical outlet.

It was perfect.

Well, it would have been, if there'd been something decent to eat in this store besides burnt popcorn.

But it was getting late. I didn't think we could be picky.

chapter 102
Turn of the Lock

I scooted out to get Metal Head and Mouse. "They've got couches! Let's go."

Mouse nodded and darted in the door. Metal Head moved slower than ever.

I got a better grip of *Green Eggs and Ham* as I waited for him to make his way inside. I was trying hard not to slobber on the cover when the door slammed.

The lock turned.

The lights flicked off.

Metal Head and Mouse were inside. And I was out.

chapter
103
The Cold, Hard Pavement

I listened to the footsteps inside the store. The furniture store employee was clearly locking up for the night. When I peeked through the window, I saw a girl with a backpack and big purple lace-up boots.

She'd already locked the back door, so she must be planning to leave from the front. I'd have to sneak in the door when she came out. Otherwise, I'd be spending the night on the cold, hard pavement while Mouse and Metal Head curled up on the couches inside.

I ran around to the front, lurking in the building's shadows. But there was a bright light shining by the door and nothing to hide behind. As I tried to figure out how to get closer without her seeing me, the girl slipped out and closed the door behind her, checking to make sure it was locked.

chapter 104
Bed Versus Couch

When the furniture store girl had driven away, I went to the window and peered in.

Metal Head was already charging in the mattress department. Mouse saw me and motioned me to come inside.

I shook my head and he ran to the window.

"I'm locked out," I barked.

Mouse's eyes widened. His little hands shot up, his fingers splayed.

"I have an idea. I'll talk you through it.

Unplug Metal Head, find some string and both of you meet me at the back door."

Mouse nodded, then took off. A few minutes later, I heard them moving around by the back door. "Did you find packing string?" I barked.

"Affirmative," Metal Head said.

"Mouse, you loop it over the lock. Metal Head, you pull one end like you did with the leash in your pen at Dogtown."

There was some scurrying and muffled words from Metal Head. "Unspool more string," I think he said.

Then a *Click-click-tchuk* and the lock slid open!

So far so good.

"Mouse, move the string to the door handle," I barked, wondering how much charge Metal Head had been able to get.

"Got it," Metal Head said.

"Now pull the door open."

I heard some clanking and groaning. The door shuddered a little.

"Do whatever you just did again," I barked.

There was more clatter, but this time the door didn't budge.

"Uh-ohhhhhh," Metal Head said.

I knew what the problem was. I could hear it in his voice. He didn't have enough charge.

"Get back to the outlet. Charge for an hour. I'll wait outside."

"Roooger, thaaaat," Metal Head drawled.

The wind whispered through the trees and it began to snow. I curled up under a bush and tried to sleep. Every few minutes I had to get up and run around to keep myself warm.

Finally, I heard them scurrying on the other side of the door.

Metal Head said something I couldn't make out.

The door groaned.

It creaked and shuddered, opened a hair, then closed again.

"Almost got it!" I barked.

More groaning and creaking, then the door opened two hairs and I wedged my nail in the opening, leaning on the door frame so I didn't fall over. Then I punched my paw through and I came flying after it.

In less than a minute, I was inside.

It was warm in the furniture store, and I was exhausted. All I could think about was: Did I want to sleep on a bed or a couch?

I dragged the book to the closest bed I could find, which happened to be in the window display. I didn't care if anyone saw me. I didn't care 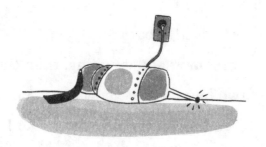 about anything. I just wanted to find a comfy spot.

Telephone Poles

I woke to the train whistle. It took me a minute to figure out where I was. The soft bed reminded me of Jessie's bed on Sycamore Avenue. I had a hard time convincing myself to get up.

When I finally did, Mouse and I got to work. We went behind the counter and began nosing around. Dogtown had cards that gave humans directions to the shelter. Would a furniture store have this?

There were no cards, but we found a pouch of brochures. Mouse pulled one out and unfolded it. On the back was a map!

The three of us looked it over. Dogtown wasn't on the map. But the river and our railroad station were, so we had our bearings. Getting home was a straight shot.

This was good news, so why did my stomach hurt? Maybe I was hungry? Or maybe it was something else. I wanted to get *Green Eggs and Ham* back to Quinn, but the thought of returning to Dogtown was making me sad.

I found myself thinking of telephone poles. Would there be telephone poles I hadn't yet checked on our way home?

chapter
106
A Heart Is a Nuisance

Luckily, Mouse had thought to wedge the spool of packing string between the door and the door jamb. Getting the door open was not nearly as difficult.

It was bitter cold when we got out, and the ground was dusted with snow. Metal Head and I took turns carrying *Green Eggs and Ham*. We were careful when we passed the book between us. We did not want it to get snowy or wet.

I saw plenty of posters along the way. None

of them had a picture of me. But they kept me going. Every time I got tired, I'd see another one up ahead.

We were walking together, me hopping, Mouse running, Metal Head clanking next to me. Then I'd see a telephone pole with a sign stapled to it and I'd hop ahead.

"I have a question for you," Metal Head said when he caught up with me. "Why are you going back?"

"I have to take the book to Quinn," I said, my paws crunching on an ice patch.

"I can do that," Metal Head said.

"I have to get dinner for Mouse," I said.

"We can find another flesh-and-blood to provide sustenance for Mouse," Metal Head said.

We walked on, watching the gusts of wind blow the new snow off the tree limbs. A car rattled behind us. A snowblower started up.

"Mouse and I have been discussing this," Metal Head said. "We wonder why you don't go home. Your humans could have called Dogtown looking for you, you know."

"They didn't," I whispered, looking back at the tracks we were making in the snow.

"What if they did and Management said you weren't there?"

"Why would Management say that?" I asked.

"Because your humans weren't searching for a three-legged dog, Chance. And that's how Management describes you."

I stopped and stared at him.

"Besides, sabbaticals aren't just six months in length. Sometimes they're nine months or a year."

I swallowed hard. How had I known the sabbatical was six months? Did the Bessers tell me that? They must have.

"For a mind made of metal, you sure have a vivid imagination," I said.

The snow started falling. Metal Head shook it off. "I'll take that as a compliment, Chance," he said.

"I guess it is," I said. "And I'll tell you something else. It isn't just empty space in there." I nosed his chest. "You have a heart."

"A heart is what Jimmy's mom would call a 'nuisance,'" Metal Head declared.

"Tell me about it," I said.

"But I don't want to trade mine in."

"Me, either." I shook the snow off my whiskers. Though right then, my heart was worn out from all the hoping. And I wasn't sure I could hope anymore.

chapter
107

Everybody Hated Mice

We were within sight of the driveway to Dogtown and the snow was starting to fall hard. Mouse had climbed on my back. He was shaking and his little feet were wet. Metal Head was worried that the snow on his coat would melt and ruin his circuitry.

We couldn't stay outside much longer, but we weren't sure how to get back in. Dogs didn't choose to go to Dogtown. Animal control brought them in. Or humans who found them on the streets or didn't want them or couldn't handle them anymore.

"You go in first," I told Metal Head. "Then Mouse can sneak in on your heels."

Mouse gestured wildly at me.

"Do you have a better plan?" I asked.

He shook his head, his whiskers sagging.

"I'll be right behind you, Mouse. They won't notice you, because they'll be busy looking at Metal Head and me. And if they spot you, I'll run interference," I told him.

Mouse was trembling all over. Management hated mice. Everybody hated mice.

We waited for a few minutes until a volunteer drove up and got out of her car. The volunteer pulled her muffler over her chin as she loped up the path.

When she got the door open, Metal Head

jumped out from behind the tree and dove in.
Then a tiny blur of brown fur sped past him.

The volunteer jumped. Front Desk's head
popped up behind the counter.

"What in the name of . . ." the volunteer
said, her eyes on Metal Head trotting by the
desk with *Green Eggs and Ham*.

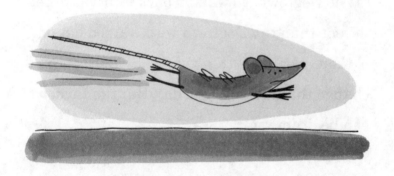

108

Humans Underestimate Dogs

The Dogtown we walked back into was different than the Dogtown we'd walked out of.

You wouldn't think a dog shelter could change that much in one day. But the turnover can be dramatic.

Sometimes an entire church group sweeps in and adopts twenty dogs. Other times, animal control brings in thirty dogs in one day.

When you're at Dogtown day in and day out,

you don't notice the changes as much as you do when you've been away.

It started with *Green Eggs and Ham*. When Front Desk saw Metal Head carrying that book, she went wackadoodle. They hadn't been able to find *Green Eggs and Ham* anywhere. It seemed impossible that Metal Head had found it.

Of course, he hadn't found it because our copy had been eaten.

"Where did he find it?" Management kept asking. "How did he know how important that book was?"

Seriously? There wasn't a dog in Dogtown who hadn't seen how important *Green Eggs and Ham* was to Quinn.

Humans underestimate dogs. They think when they say: *Sit, Lie Down, Roll Over* and we don't comply, it's because we don't understand. If humans went around telling other humans to *Sit, Lie Down, and Roll Over*, do you think they'd do it?

Never.

chapter 109
Walk of Shame

Management took photos of Metal Head with *Green Eggs and Ham* and put them on the Dogtown website. They got Metal Head a brand-new Reading Buddy sweater. And gave him a permanent pen on Reading Buddy Row.

In all the fuss about Metal Head, they ignored me, which was fine. I don't begrudge Metal Head the attention.

There was no way I could explain that it had

been Mouse who had found the book.

I was just trying to adjust to the idea that Dogtown was my forever home when I felt the snap of a leash on my collar. "I'll tell you one thing, Chance, you're never going to run away again," Management said, her face grumpy and wrinkled as a bloodhound's. She marched me down the walk of shame to the basement.

So that's how it was.

Metal Head was a genius. And I was a bad dog.

That night I was so hungry I had a hard time leaving kibble for Mouse. But I knew his brothers and sisters would be hungry, too. So, I set aside seven kibbles. Then I licked my bowl. And licked it again. Then a third time because why not?

In some ways I was happy to be back. I'd complained about the basement being cold, but compared to the snow outside it really wasn't bad. Anyhoo, placement in the basement was

temporary. There were consequences to running away, but they wouldn't last long. I was Management's lucky dog. She needed me.

That night, up high in the rafters in the dim light of the one bulb up there, I saw the shadow of Mouse acting out our journey for his sisters and brothers. He performed the whole thing, culminating with the moment he stole the shrimp.

When he was done, all his siblings clapped their little hands, and I yipped my appreciation. I was grateful for my friends at Dogtown, but I couldn't stop thinking about what Metal Head had said. Was it possible Professor Besser's sabbatical wasn't six months? Was it possible it had lasted for one year?

Mouse was more worried I'd been sent to the basement than I was. After he finished his performance, he brought out the deck of cards and put the five of hearts in my chain-link fence.

He was sure that would get me out of there. It had worked so well before.

But in the morning Management took out the card and locked the deck up. It was an old trick and it didn't work anymore.

I would have to wait until the Wednesday

night poker game rolled around. Then I'd be
Management's lucky dog and I'd get the run of
the place again.

chapter 111

A Place in His Heart

When a metal dog misbehaves, they blame the manufacturer.

When a real dog misbehaves, they blame the dog.

Even so, Metal Head hadn't chosen to be *the genius*. It was Management who'd made that call. Was it possible that metal dogs couldn't help who they were, any more than we could?

I no longer believed Metal Head was a hopeless boohoo, either. Now I thought he was a courageous dog who had returned to Jimmy's house to find out what had happened.

It had been a painful journey, but when it was over, there was a place in that dog's heart for Quinn that hadn't been there before.

chapter 112
Waiting

The hours moved slowly in the basement. The hardest part of living down there was being separated from Metal Head. He'd earned himself a space on Reading Buddy Row. And because Metal Head was up there and I was in the basement, I would not get to see Quinn either.

But Reading Buddy day came and went. No Quinn.

When Wednesday finally rolled around, I

was pretty excited. This would be my last afternoon in the basement.

After dinner, I waited by my gate for Management to arrive.

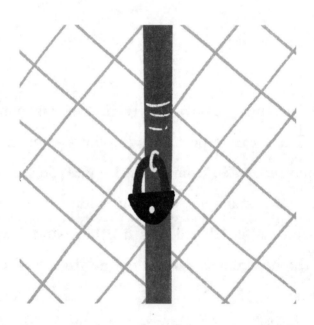

chapter
113
Bear

Management never came.

I soon found out why. When I was gone, Bear, the Jack Russell, had taken my spot under the poker table.

Management had won big that night. So Bear was the dog who got to go to poker night.

He was her lucky dog.

Not me.

chapter
114
Bootlicker

Bear was a bootlicker. A lot of us were boot-lickers, but did he have to be a great Reading Buddy and a lucky poker dog, too?

Even though Bear had the run of the place, he stayed close to Management. He followed her wherever she went. And if he spotted anything out of order, he would yip in Management's face until Management saw it, too.

Management really liked that. I could tell.

So Bear was off the books. And I was on them.

My luck had finally run out.

chapter 115

My Affairs in Order

There I was in the basement, dreaming of blueberry pancakes.

I'd imagine myself curled up in Jessie's fuzzy blanket, my head resting on her leg, only to find I was cuddling my water dish. In my dreams I smelled the rich grass, pine trees, and potting soil of Sycamore Avenue. I stood on the porch, barking to protect the humans I loved.

I'd wake up and there Mouse would be, staring down at me, his whiskers sagging.

I realized then that I had to get my affairs in order. Who would feed Mouse when I was gone? Metal Head said he would find a flesh-and-blood to help, but I didn't know if he had.

I managed to get a message to Metal Head with Trooper who had had a short stint in the basement for swallowing a hose bib. My message said Metal Head would need to make sure there was always a flesh-and-blood who would share her kibbles with Mouse.

Then a little blessing came my way. Mr. Molinari came down to the basement with Management. "Would it be possible," Mr. Molinari asked, "for the metal dog to be put in the same pen where he was before? Quinn likes consistency. He's used to running down here. I want to make sure his first day back goes off without a hitch."

"Of course," Management said. "I'm glad

to hear Quinn's coming back. You know, the weirdest thing happened. Remember how we couldn't find the book Quinn liked?"

"*Green Eggs and Ham*," Mr. Molinari said.

"Right. You'll never guess who found it."

"The metal dog?" Mr. Molinari said.

"How did you know?" Management asked.

"Just a hunch." Mr. Molinari stroked his sideburns. "Where'd he come from anyway?"

"He was a donation. They all are."

"He isn't a standard brand," Mr. Molinari said.

"No. He looks like a do-it-yourself job. Somebody's pet project, I bet."

Mr. Molinari nodded. "I'll tell you what. There's something more to that dog than just wires and circuits."

Management leaned down to pet Bear. "I

know what you mean. He really seemed to understand Quinn."

"This is why I love teaching. You never can tell what will reach a kid. There's an element of wonder to it all, you know?" Mr. Molinari said as they walked away.

chapter
116
Littermates for Life

Metal Head was as happy to see me as I was to see him.

Friendship is mysterious. I have dog friends who look like me, but the friendship doesn't last. There's no glue holding us together.

Then along comes a tiny rodent and a metal dog . . . as different from me as it's possible to be. And we're littermates for life.

chapter
117

Left Shoe Untied

The next Reading Buddy day, we were all waiting for Quinn to arrive.

When I heard his feet thunder down the stairs, I felt like my heart was going to bust out my chest. There he was with his crooked glasses, his star shirt, and the laces of his left shoe untied. He slid up in front of Metal Head's pen and did a break-dance of pure joy.

Then he got *Green Eggs and Ham* and danced again.

Quinn plopped down next to Metal Head. First, they read the old way: Metal Head saying the words and Quinn turning the pages.

Then they read it the new way: Metal Head turning the pages and Quinn saying the words.

It was so quiet in the basement you could hear a kibble drop.

Even the flesh-and-bloods had grown to admire Metal Head. He was the dog who devised the plan to save Geraldine. He was the dog who memorized *Green Eggs and Ham*. And he was the dog who Quinn had chosen.

Right then a lot of the animosity we had for metal dogs began to melt away. Metal Head was a robot dog and we liked him. He was different than the other robot dogs. But still.

Respect is a powerful thing, you know?

chapter 118

A Dog's Superpower

One snowy day a few weeks later, animal control brought in seventeen dogs. They were all skinny, scruffy, and full of fleas. Apparently, they'd lived in a trailer park with a human who had become too old and frail to live on his own. He moved in with his daughter, who let him bring just one dog.

The other seventeen went to us.

Dogtown had been full even before the dogs

arrived. With seventeen new dogs, there was simply no room.

Management and Front Desk were walking through the basement trying to figure out where to put the new dogs.

"What about Chance? We could use her pen tonight."

"She ran away when we let her out," Management said.

"Yeah, but I heard she only got as far as the parking lot," Front Desk said.

That wasn't true. Humans are always telling stories about dogs. Toto, the Big Red Dog, the Lady and the Tramp . . . you think those stories really happened?

"Anyway," Front Desk continued, "it's snowing pretty hard. She won't leave in the middle of a blizzard. What should we do?"

Management nodded. "She's on the top of

the list. I suppose it doesn't make much difference."

Front Desk sighed. "The longer I'm here, the
more attached I get to these dogs."

Management came in my pen, squatted
down, and ran her hand over my fur. "Dogs
have that effect on all of us. You have a bad day,
shoot your mouth off, spend the rent money on
lottery tickets, they don't care. They love you
no matter what. That's their superpower."

"Love?"

"Yeah, they have such big hearts."

"So why do we . . ." Front Desk let her sentence trail off.

Management sighed. "We don't have the room. I've got the board raising money for a new addition. Fifty more pens."

"I didn't know that. That's great!" Front Desk smiled.

Management nodded. "But that won't help Chance." She tipped her glasses up and buried her face in her hands.

Management was a good petter. One of the best, actually. And I liked that bit about a dog's superpower is love. Even so, the facts were clear.

My life at Dogtown was over.

chapter 119

A Page from His Manual

Right after that, a new recruit was put in my old cage. And I was allowed to walk free in Dogtown again.

"This is your chance, Chance," Metal Head said.

I didn't even mind that Metal Head had used my name that way because what he said was true.

Mouse nodded. He made his sign for home.

"I'll take good care of Mouse. Make sure he

gets fed," Metal Head said, tearing a page from his manual and handing it to me.

It wasn't printed, the way the other pages were. It was a page he'd written himself.

It said: *Your heart is a muscle. It grows stronger the more you use it.*

chapter
120
Tucked Under My Collar

I didn't see how Metal Head's words could apply to a metal dog. Maybe it was what Professor Besser called a "metaphor."

Or maybe it was true. Could it be that Metal Head's heart was a muscle the way ours is?

Mouse folded the page, tucked it under my collar, and I choked out a goodbye.

I'd lived long enough to know how rare it is to find friends like Metal Head and Mouse, and I didn't want to leave them.

chapter
121
Lopsided Moon

I headed to the front door. It was poker night. Bear was already under the poker table. And lots of volunteers were coming in the door. I waited behind the front desk until two ladies in puffy parkas came in together.

"You think he's cute," the volunteer in the blue parka said.

Blue parka rolled her eyes. "I do not."

"Oh, come on. You are so busted. I've seen you stare at him. You're like—" White Parka stopped, cocked her head, and batted her eye-lashes.

They were so busy teasing each other that they didn't notice me slip out the door.

Outside there was a big yellow lopsided moon, an owl hooting in the trees, and icy snowdrifts by the side of the road.

This time, I knew where I was going. After all the walks I'd taken with Jessie and Pro-fessor Besser, I knew the south side of town very well.

chapter
122
A Foolish Idea

Just because the dictionary said a sabbatical was six months, didn't mean every sabbatical was six months, did it?

I hated that I was full of hope. Once hope gets inside you, you want your wishes to come true so badly, you just can't imagine that they won't.

Even knowing this, I could not convince myself that this was a foolish idea.

Metal Head said I had to hope more, not less.

That I had to find out what happened. That my heart would grow stronger because I tried, not from the results of what I did. It was my effort that made it stronger.

The odds of this working out were slim, just as they had been for Metal Head. Even if the sabbatical had been one year long, the Bessers would have been home by now. So why hadn't they come looking for me?

chapter
123
Sycamore Avenue

Every time I saw a headlight, I jumped. The dog-sitter's boyfriend would not be searching for me, but I was still scared.

I stayed away from the headlights, the car doors, and the icy spots. I hopped fast to keep warm and licked the snow when I got thirsty.

My heart began to beat faster as I got closer. The streets were so familiar, the meowing cats in the corner house, the rich cinnamon and nutmeg smells of the turban lady's house, the *ba da ba da shing* of the girl practicing her drums.

It felt so good to be back on Sycamore Avenue. It was almost like I had four legs again.

When I got to number seventeen, the light was on!

I scanned the driveway for the dog-sitter's small white car and the dog-sitter's boyfriend's big blue truck.

They weren't there.

But neither was the professor's station wagon.

chapter 124
Home

I hopped up the path to the porch.

The wicker chairs had not been covered.

The flyers on the doorknob had not been collected.

The snow on the path had not been shoveled.

No one was home.

chapter 125

The Great Dog Park in the Sky

I ran around the yard peeing on every bush. Then I curled up in my favorite spot under the porch swing and fell into a deep sleep.

The next morning when I woke up the driveway was still empty. The house still deserted. The porch covered with ice.

I was stiff with cold, my mouth dry, my bones achy. I melted snow on my tongue and kept waiting. I didn't know what else to do.

By mid-morning, it was warmer, and

comforting smells filled the air: the wood-burning stove next door, the corn bread baking across the street, the sunbaked bicycle grease smell of the porch.

This was home. If I was going to the great dog park in the sky, I wanted to leave from here.

chapter 126

A Left Ear Scratch

I heard a delivery truck pull into the driveway. A man with dreads and purple glasses jumped out. He wore a brown uniform and smelled like Doublemint gum.

Dikembe! I loved Dikembe, the UPS driver who left packages for the professor.

I wagged my tail.

"Chance! Where you been, girl?" Dikembe reached in his coat pocket for a biscuit.

I swallowed it whole as Dikembe carried

a large suitcase up the stairs and rolled it to the door. He reached in his pocket for another biscuit. "Cold out here for you," Dikembe said, scratching behind my left ear.

I like a left ear scratch better than a right ear scratch and Dikembe remembered that.

"You okay here?" he asked, but I wasn't paying attention to him right then because I had sniffed something.

I stared at the suitcase. Even with all the new smells—airplane exhaust, garlic bread,

Doublemint gum—I caught the aroma of toasted almonds and manila folders.

PROFESSOR J. BESSER, the tag said.

I crawled onto the suitcase and curled up, happier than I had been for a very long time.

It was only after Dikembe left that I began thinking about what Management had said about me.

Nobody wants a dog with three legs.

Blueberry Pancakes

It was late afternoon when a strange car pulled into the driveway. It wasn't the dog-sitter's car or the dog-sitter's boyfriend's truck or the Bessers' station wagon.

I jumped up and began barking.

The car door opened, and I heard a shout.

"Chance!" Jessie cried, a blue knit cap pulled down low. "Mom, it's Chance!"

"Honey, that's not possible," the professor

said as she struggled to unload suitcases from the trunk.

"It *is* her! Look, Mom, look!" Jessie tore up the steps two at a time. When she reached me, she buried her face in my fur and tenderly whispered my name.

She smelled of blueberry pancakes, pink bubble gum, and coconut shampoo.

"She came home, Mom!" Jessie whispered.

The professor let the suitcase fall to the ground as the man in the car waved and drove away.

"For goodness' sake," the professor murmured.

Then we were all hugging, and I inhaled the sweet scents of the humans I loved: toasted almonds, manila folders, and blueberry pancakes all together again.

"I told you that picture of the dog in the furniture store . . . the one on Nextdoor . . . I told you it was her," Jessie said.

"I don't see how that's possible." Professor Besser scratched behind my left ear. "The dog-sitter emailed me she'd run away in January. That was almost a year ago."

"Maybe she lived in the furniture store. Or maybe she was waiting here for us that whole time." Jessie kissed the top of my head.

"The dog-sitter was here until a few days ago. She would have told us if Chance had come back."

"She's cold, Mom. Look she's shivering." Jessie pulled me closer.

"Let's get her inside," the professor said.

But I didn't want to go inside. If I moved from the suitcase, they'd see I only had three legs.

Time to go in, sweet dog," Professor Besser said.

I stalled, waiting for them to turn around. There was no way to jump off the suitcase without them seeing me.

Jessie got her purple plastic wheeler bag and bumped it up the stairs to the porch. The professor half-carried, half-dragged her last suitcase in the door.

Then they waited for me.

"Chance, you're home," Jessie said.

There was nothing I could do.

I took a deep breath then leapt off the suit-case and dashed by them hopping as fast as I could.

The professor gasped. "Jessie!" she said. "Chance is missing a leg!"

Jessie came closer, inspecting my stump. "Chance! What happened to you?"

If Mouse were here, maybe he could perform the story for them. But I didn't have hands the way he did. All I could think to do was my act.

The tri-pawed juggle.

The hug and snuggle.

A dog plays dead.

A ball on my head.

And a one-pawed spin.

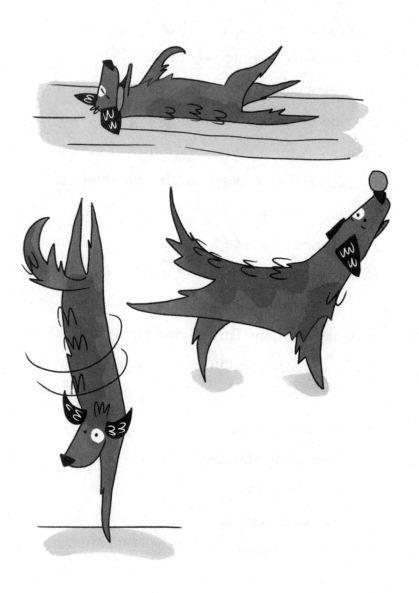

chapter 129

New Tricks

She's learned new tricks," Jessie said, "but why's she doing them now?"

"She's singing for her supper." Professor Besser sat down on the floor and ran her hand over my head. "Good job, Chance, but you don't need to perform for us," she whispered.

"We have to take her to the vet," Jessie said.

"We'll get her checked out, but it looks like she's doing just fine with three legs."

Jessie stroked my neck. "Hey, there's

something under her collar," she said, pulling out Metal Head's note.

"*Your heart is a muscle*," Jessie read aloud. "*It grows stronger the more you use it*."

"I wonder who wrote that?"

"One of Chance's friends," Jessie said.

Professor Besser laughed.

Jessie's hands flew to her hips. "She could have friends, you don't know."

"You're right about that, Jessie Besser. I do not know," Professor Besser said.

About then, I lost control of my licking. I licked the both of them from head to foot. And when I was done, I licked them all over again.

The Smell of Ink

We missed you so much, Chance."

I lost count of how many times Jessie said those words that day. But I never tired of hearing them.

At Dogtown, I'd seen plenty of humans give up their dogs. I knew the posture, the cold, hard stares, the clipped voices, the fast walk away without looking back.

The Bessers were not acting like they were going to give me up. They were behaving like the happy families who leave Dogtown with a new puppy.

That evening, I lay on Jessie's bed—oh, how I'd missed that beautiful bed!—and watched her unpack.

I liked seeing Jessie's clothes. And smelling the Jessie smells I'd forgotten. Peanuts, chocolate fudge sauce, laundry detergent, and an ink smell coming from the bottom of her bag. What was that?

I peered down at the suitcase. There under Jessie's hairbrush was a poster with my photo on it.

MISSING BROWN-AND-WHITE DOG it read, in Jessie's careful printing.

chapter
131
Three Friends

If people ask what happened to me, the professor and Jessie always said: "Our dog ran away from the dog-sitter. When we came back a whole year later, she was waiting for us on the doorstep. She was skinny, she was shivering, and she'd lost a leg."

The Bessers never tire of telling that story.

And most humans who hear it walk away searching their pockets for a tissue.

But then, dog park humans are like that. Mush balls in spandex . . .

Even so, the tale is true. Their short version. And my long one.

But what's it all mean?

I think it's about how hard it is to operate that thumping thing in your chest. (A manual is not such a bad idea, you know?)

And how nice it is to have besties who are beasties not the least bit like me. I wouldn't trade all the Milk-Bones in Michigan for Mouse and Metal Head. I will miss them, but I'll find a way to visit. The border collie in me is resourceful. The Aussie is persistent. Luck helps a lot, too.

Didn't I tell you three legs were lucky?

Three friends? That's lucky, too.

7 Things Kids Can Do to Help Shelter Dogs

1. Be a matchmaker. How cool to be the person who helps a dog find her new home. You could make that happen by sharing cute photos of your local shelter dogs with kids and grown-ups you know. Enthusiasm is powerful stuff.

2. Be the dog whisperer. If your dog steals the turkey, eats the stuffing, chews the silverware, and slobbers on the napkins, she won't be popular at your house. Help your family train your dog. A well-trained dog is less likely to end up at a shelter.

3. Be super powerful. Write thank-you notes and bake cookies for your local shelter volunteers, so they feel appreciated for their hard work. Getting thanked by a kid is the best thing ever.

4. Be the fun human. Waiting in line, waiting in traffic, waiting outside the principal's office . . . not fun, right? That's how it feels to be a shelter dog waiting for a home. Donate dog food, dog toys, or shelter-approved chew toys to your shelter and make a dog's day.

5. Be a foster mom or dad. Ask your parents if you can "foster" a dog or cat. Providing a temporary home for an animal grants you automatic superhero status.

6. Be a dog's best friend.
   Fill water dishes, feed,
   bathe, brush, and be the
   world's best belly rubber.
   There's nothing better than
   giving doggy love.

7. Be the kid with the good
   idea. Suggest a field trip to
   your local dog shelter. The more kids
   (and adults) know about dog shelters,
   the better cared for the pets in your town
   will be.

Acknowledgments

Dogtown would not exist without the incredible team from Feiwel and Friends/Macmillan. A big sloppy dog kiss to Jean Feiwel, our dog-loving publisher. And to Liz Szabla who has infinite patience and an uncanny instinct for how to make a text a whole lot better. Thank you for taking loving care of Geraldine, Buster, Chance, Metal Head, and Mouse.

The copyeditors Helen Seachrist and Amber Williams, bless you for catching our mistakes.

The creative director Rich Deas who had a clear idea for how this book should look and the skill to bring that vision to the pages of *Dogtown*. And to the incredibly talented Wallace West whose wry

342

humor, originality, and heart brought the book to life.

The MCPG marketing and publicity team who got the word out about our book. *Dogtown* would be a book sitting in a box somewhere without you.

The powerhouse sales team who worked so hard to get *Dogtown* into the hands of kids.

Our agents: Elena Giovinazzo (Pippin Properties) and Elizabeth Harding (Curtis, Brown) who have never steered us wrong.

Mary Cate Stevenson and Noah Nofz (Two Cats Communication) who help us navigate the roller-coaster ride of our careers.

To the Rogue Colors, Sharon Levin, Teri Sloat, and Katharine Otoshi for being great friends and providing much-needed support these last few years.

To Lauren Cole and everyone at Marin Humane and the shelters everywhere (and to all the humans who work or volunteer at shelters!) for doing their best to make sure every dog finds a loving home.

And to Katherine's pack: Michael, Clara, and Julia. And Gennifer's pack—they know who they are.

But our biggest thanks go to the teachers and librarians who handled the unprecedented challenges of 2020, 2021, and 2022 with grace and dignity. And the booksellers who worked tirelessly to deliver books to readers in these exceedingly difficult times. You are the unsung heroes of our time.

Thank you for reading this Feiwel & Friends book.
The friends who made *Dogtown* possible are:

Jean Feiwel, Publisher

Liz Szabla, VP, Associate Publisher

Rich Deas, Senior Creative Director

Holly West, Senior Editor

Anna Roberto, Executive Editor

Kat Brzozowski, Senior Editor

Dawn Ryan, Executive Managing Editor

Kim Waymer, Senior Production Manager

Emily Settle, Editor

Rachel Diebel, Editor

Foyinsi Adegbonmire, Editor

Brittany Groves, Assistant Editor

Helen Seachrist, Senior Production Editor

Follow us on Facebook or visit us online
at mackids.com. Our books are friends for life.